Translated from the Greek by Helen Cavanagh

History of a Vendetta

Yorgi Yatromanolakis

Dedalus / Hippocrene

Funded by the
EC-Brussels

*For Nicholas, who is learning to read and write
and many other things besides.*

Published in the UK by Dedalus Ltd,
Langford Lodge, St Judith's Lane, Sawtry, Cambs, PE17 5XE

UK ISBN 0 946626 74 X

Published in the USA by Hippocrene Books Inc,
171, Madison Avenue, New York, NY10016

US ISBN 0 7818 0002 1

Distributed in Canada by Marginal Distribution,
Unit 103, 277 George Street, Peterborough, Ontario, KJ9 3G9

First published in Greece as Istoria in 1982
First English edition 1991

Istoria copyright©Yorgi Yatromanolakis 1982
Translation copyright©Dedalus 1991

A C.I.P. listing for this title is available on request.

Cover picture is 'The Reckless Sleeper' by Rene Magritte©ADAGP, Paris
and DACS , London 1992.
Reproduced by courtesy of the Tate Gallery London.

Dedalus would like to thank the Commission of the European Community
for funding the translation of this work into English.

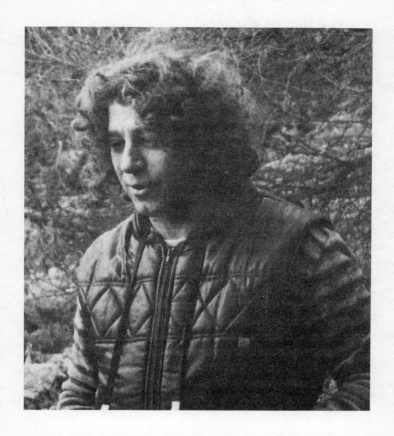

Yorgi Yatromanolakis was born in 1940 on the Greek Island of Crete. He read Philosophy at Athens University before doing a Ph.D. at King's College, London in Classics. He is now Professor of Classics at Athens University.

The publication of History of a Vendetta, his third novel, established him as one of Greece's most important 20th century novelists. It was awarded the first Greek National Prize for Literature and the Nikos Kazantzakis Prize for Literature.

'This is what I saw for myself and my own opinion and history.'

(Herodotus II.99.1)

DEDALUS EUROPE 1992

At the end of 1992 the 12 Member States of the EEC will inaugurate an open market which Dedalus is celebrating with a major programme of new translations from the 8 languages of the EEC into English . The new translations will reflect the whole range of Dedalus' publishing programme : classics, literary fantasy and contemporary fiction.

Titles so far selected are :

From French :

The Devil in Love - Jacques Cazotte
Smarra & Trilby - Charles Nodier
Angels of Perversity - Remy de Gourmont
Le Calvaire - Octave Mirbeau
The Dedalus Book of French Fantasy - editor Christine Donougher

From German:

The Angel of the West Window - Gustav Meyrink
The Green Face - Gustav Meyrink
The Architect of Ruins - Herbert Rosendorfer
The Dedalus Book of Austrian Fantasy: the Meyrink Years 1890-1930 - editor Mike Mitchell
The Dedalus Book of German Fantasy: the Romantics and Beyond - editor Maurice Raraty

From Italian :

Senso (and other stories) - Camillo Boito
One, Nobody and One Hundred Thousand - Luigi Pirandello

THE TRANSLATOR

Helen Cavanagh was born in Athens in 1947. She was educated at Athens University and King's College, London. She combines a career as a lawyer in England with translating works of fiction, art and architecture.

TRANSLATOR'S NOTE

The feast of the Dormition, corresponds to the Assumption of the Virgin Mary in the western church, and is celebrated on 15th August. According to Greek Orthodox legend, the Virgin did not die but fell asleep and was carried up to heaven by the angels. It is a favourite subject of Byzantine iconography and is still a major annual feast throughout Greece.

A

When Emmanuel Zervos, son of George, aged fifty two, was shot low in the stomach at dawn on Wednesday 8th August 1928, there was no witness other than the murderer. The murderer observed that Zervos felt great surprise as his cummerbund suddenly came undone and he lost all physical contact with the ground. The law of gravity which, as they say, holds in place all objects, animals and men, was overturned so that a vacuum was formed between the earth and the victim's knees, one that must have been two metres high, perhaps more. Although Zervos was in the prime of his life, he didn't think to stretch his arms to the ground and protect himself from the fall. On the contrary, after hovering for some time at a great height, he crashed onto the dirt-track in the vineyard with his head hanging on the vines. For two or three hours he lay there motionless, bleeding, and it was in this position that he was finally found. So not only did he fail to recover the money he was owed, but he also lost among the thick dust all the coins he was carrying in his belt. These were, one English gold sovereign with the king's head facing left, a silver twenty-drachma piece of the Greek Republic depicting a woman among ears of grain, two nickel talira with the picture of an owl, seven drachma pieces and three or more little twenty-lepta coins which were worn round the edges.

On the following Tuesday 14th August, the eve of the Dormition, at eight o'clock in the morning, Grigoris Dikeakis, son of the murderer Pavlos, stood over the spot where Zervos had fallen, holding the harvest basket. He kicked at the dried blood with his boot and this brought to light the gold sovereign, the silver twenty-drachma, the two nickel talira and four drachmas. The rest of the coins were lost forever. Grigoris, who had found Zervos lying face down in their vineyard seven days ago, was impressed by this fresh discovery; even more so, because for the first time in the twenty seven years of his life he held such a large sum in his hands. He calculated that this money more than covered the damage done by the dead man as he fell on top of the vines, as well as anything else destroyed in their vineyard by the people who, moved by necessity or curiosity, had gathered round Zervos as soon as the crime became known.

It so happened, however, that the murderer's son experienced something that has been observed many times: certain people, although they themselves have never committed any crime or injustice, still feel that their kinship with the perpetrator of a crime puts them in a difficult and, at times, annoying position. It is said moreover that if they find themselves at the place where the crime was committed, their annoyance and disquiet is even greater, because a given place may not only contribute to a criminal act but it can repeatedly recall that crime to one's memory. So given that the damage to the vineyard was not great, what had to be done now was to pick the grapes - beginning with the one hundred and forty three vines of sultanas on the right side of the track. To the left, the seventy nine vines of currants did not yet need picking; but because the weather in August is known for its instability and can bring heavy and destructive rains, Grigoris thought it wiser to make haste and do what had to be done on his own, as his father was a fugitive from justice.

The little house at the end of the dirt-track where the vineyard ends was completely intact, although Zervos had been shot from there, as the murderer himself asserted ten days after the crime. In fact during the reconstruction of the murder, on Saturday 18th August, the murderer insisted that when he saw a shadow approach the house from the road, he had pushed the gun out of the little barred window beside the door and fired. Dikeakis, who was often called Dikeos - 'Righteous' - both as an abbreviation of his real name and also because he often spoke up for his rights, was not believed at the time. But during the trial it was finally accepted that he had fired straight ahead from the window - not from a nearby fence after lying in wait, as was claimed in the initial police report.

Grigoris asked himself once more where his father might be and he had no doubt that, even if a murder does not change a place, it does change, and radically so, the people involved in it: the murderer, the victim, and almost all their relatives. Therefore, by having to flee from justice, the murderer creates trouble for his own people as well as for the victim's relatives, as they all search for him, each for their own reasons. In turn, the murderer himself not only loses his regular home, but his diet changes, he goes to bed in one place and in the morning he gets up in another, unties his belt and relieves himself. In the case of Dikeos, who was accustomed to wandering round the vineyard from dawn to dusk, slept there and relieved himself there, the change was enormous, as he was to say time and time again.

Zervos naturally underwent a greater change. The bullet from the Mannlicher that killed him, however well polished and oiled by Dikeos, and however small a hole it made initially, nevertheless pierced the skin with force, entered the stomach and ruptured those vital organs which help with digestion and defecation, and finally came out making a bigger hole low in his back and breaking two vertebrae in the process. After continuous and prolonged bleeding and loss of acids, the man's body was drained and his soul (which is said to resemble the silk moth and live a little higher up in the diaphragm) fell and drowned in the still liquids, the thick blood and the bile. The only living things that Grigoris found circling round Zervos' body were several flies, the sort which are born when a man dies. But inside the murdered man's nostril was a dead fly: black, small, with big wings - the fly that lives and moves inside the blood of the living, but when their blood pours out, it too dries up and comes to an end.

Grigoris was stabbed much later, three years and three months, to be precise, in November 1931, sometime between the feasts of St. Minas and the Beheading of St. Catherine. He saw then his own entrails pour out into the river, having been stabbed by the son of the victim, Markos Zervos, son of Emmanuel. It was then that he called to mind once more the killing of Zervos, although the place was different. Then he examined life and passed judgement on it with the speed that characterises only those about to die and especially those who have been stabbed. His final judgement is of no interest. What is important is that Grigoris cut and compressed time so that its pace quickened and its span was shortened. From the month of November, when severe cold descends from the mountain and the constellations of Winter are in the ascent, Dikeos' son withdrew to the hot month of August, three whole years earlier. Lying half in the river and half on the bank, he heard again the flies which are born when a man dies and felt in his nostrils the fluttering of the black fly which has wings of gold and of iron, which takes a man up and lifts him two or three metres high, sometimes more, and then drops him crashing to the ground, dead.

By making time contract and expand in this manner, Grigoris found himself alive again in their vineyard on Tuesday, eve of the Dormition. He picked the grapes off four vines, began on the fifth but stopped, exhausted, with the adequate excuse that the change which sometimes comes after a killing had taken place in himself as well. The fact that it was he who first saw Zervos, heard the flies and smelled the air around the corpse, carried him home and held the wake in his house, all contributed to this change. He had heard that the terrible act of murder has an evil influence on the living for the same number of years that they have lived up to the moment of the deed. The murderer's son calculated that for him it would last another twenty seven years, and this thought rather depressed him. He did not think it serious that his father might suffer for fifty one years in the future, because a murderer is probably subject to different rules. He decided then to stop picking grapes for the moment and, because he felt heavy after many days' lack of sleep, he hoped to have a rest in the coolness of the little house.

Once inside, he first looked over and counted all their tools, as his grandfather had taught him, without pointing to them or speaking aloud, but silently in his mind: the big hoe, the small hoe, the crowbar, the pick, the rake, the bill-hook, the sickle, the spray, the four baskets, the big bucket for diluting the potassium, the eight sacks for the dry raisins and the coil of wire for catching the hare, the fox and the badger. He then thought that, if all tools have some power because they contain within them the fire and metal of the earth, then his father's rifle, the family Mannlicher, must possess even more power and more heat. Other tools may be made from fire, but a rifle can produce fire. Its metal is heated to a very high temperature, it hardens, dries out and becomes light.

This is why when someone uses a Mannlicher, having previously polished and cleaned the tip of the bullet, that bullet not only finds its target but is automatically attracted by the heat of the human body and pierces the skin, the flesh and the bones in a manner described as 'humane'.

On the morning of 18th August, on the eve of the general elections, after the feast of the Dormition was over, Dikeos was caught with his cummerbund undone, relieving himself among the carob trees. When they asked him why he had polished and cleaned the five bullets they found on him, he gave a whole series of answers which began chronologically from the basic processing of metals as they come out of the earth in crude form, and ended in the Spring of 1916 when he was still serving in Venizelos' police force in Free Thessaloniki together with Zervos. Dikeos explained that a clean bullet is better than a rusty one and that in order for a rifle to be effective it has to be humane, and he repeated his whole theory. As for the sixth bullet in the Mannlicher's chamber, he said it must have dissolved inside Zervos' body; and as for the spent cartridge, it must have shot out of the little window and got lost in the vineyard.

The cartridge, however, was found among the bed clothes by Grigoris on Thursday 9th August, the day of Zervos' funeral. After it was established from other sources that Dikeos was the murderer, Grigoris walked to the vineyard, opened the little house and discovered the cartridge. He noticed that it was slightly black at the rim, but the cap had been struck by the bolt exactly at the centre, because this rifle of theirs was perfect, always well oiled and clean and it never jammed. Grigoris took the empty cartridge, smelled it, as he did with all cartridges, and put it in the inside pocket of his waistcoat.

14

It was there that he also put Zervos' money: the sovereign, the twenty-drachma piece, the talira and the drachmas.

In November 1931, while they were preparing Grigoris' dead, blood-stained body for burial (as such things must be done and as the church teaches and custom dictates), they found in the inside pocket of his waistcoat the clean and polished cartridge, together with one sovereign and nine drachmas. Zervos' relatives did not claim this money, not so much because Markos was Grigoris' murderer, as because they did not know that it came from a member of their family. After all, the same thing would have happened even before Grigoris' death, considering that Zervos' family had filed many lawsuits against Dikeos and his son, on the initiative and advice of their lawyer. Those who dressed Grigoris handed the money to the treasurer of the church council, as there was no immediate claimant, and it covered the expenses for the funeral and for the murdered man's memorial service in three months' time.

Grigoris sat on his father's bed and looked at the world through the open window. He saw the dirt-track which divided their vineyard in two, the neighbour's harvested field, the fence with the wild roses, and the slope leading to the main road. It was this road which took him straight to his village.

The village was situated between two cemeteries: an old Turkish one and a new Christian one. For it is said that while the two peoples, Greeks and Turks, are alive, they can sit, eat and drink together, but when they die they must not be buried together, because no one knows the precise limits or the jurisdictions of the Christian or Turkish saints. It is known that the site of a graveyard corresponds with another place hidden inside the earth, two or three hundred metres deep; so it is sensible to have separated the places of burial already on the surface. The Turkish graveyard was now abandoned, as their people had long since gone. During the first Exchange of Populations in 1913, when Grigoris was twelve and his grandfather was still alive, the Turks took away in clean white sacks the bones of those who had died long before and whose flesh had completely decayed. Those who had died recently were left in the village cemetery, and no one paid them the customary rites or looked after them or visited them; but then no one disturbed them in any way either. The Greek cemetery, where Grigoris stopped, had more graves; they were built above ground, sometimes lined with marble, like Zervos' grave, with a little cubicle in front for the oil lamp and an icon of the saint who helps the dead man avenge his wrongs and intercedes for his sins.

Zervos' protector was St. Eleftherios - 'the Liberator' - who, according to legend, delivered people from evil and injustice; also, according to the followers of Eleftherios Venizelos, the saint had played a role in the liberation of the island itself. In that same graveyard was buried Grigoris' grandfather, who was killed by a fall in 1916. But his saint was a different one. In their house they kept the icon of St. Michael the Leader of Armies, the sword-bearer, the measurer of justice, holding the scales in his hand. Michael is no mere saint but an archangel, fierce and implacable, so he did no favours, nor did he intercede for anyone. This was clearly shown to be true not only by the death of old Dikeakis but also by his first visit to their house in November 1901 when he found Grigoris' mother Maria in the last stages of labour.

Now during Grigoris' birth, as he learned later, a great battle was fought between Maria (who was called 'the Quiet One' because she spoke and walked quietly) and the Leader of Armies: they pulled the baby out by his right leg and this is why it was two fingers longer than the other when he walked. But when Grigoris walked inside his mind, stepping a whole metre above the earth without falling or stumbling anywhere, his legs were of the same length and well balanced. He could go from their vineyard to the village and back fifty or sixty times and his legs never missed their footing nor did he limp, even though he was a cripple. He used to stop, however, by the side of the road, so he wouldn't get too tired, and watch people pass him either on foot or on donkeys; he watched the domestic animals, the dogs (who were at once both wild and tame), sometimes a badger, a fox or a hare. And neither man nor beast ever saw him, not even the farm dog who races through the valley sniffing everywhere and creating turmoil. But if the dog of the mind happens to pass the spot where Grigoris is sitting, it sees him; and if it races a hare or chases a fox into the open, jumping over fences and ditches and dashing from one corner of the mind to the other, then the head gets heavy; this was why Grigoris would sometimes fall asleep as he was eating or working in the fields. Then Dikeos would shout loudly and Grigoris would wake up in alarm.

Although his father worked hard, slept little and deliberated endlessly about justice and injustice, he never amassed any capital like Zervos. Indeed they had both served as volunteer soldiers and later in Venizelos' civil guard in mainland Greece, but this was no reason for them both to make a fortune. Because capital may grow by itself, like a silkworm that feeds in its sleep spreading itself on its frame as it eats and digests the mulberry leaf; but first it has to be born. That is to say when someone, for example Zervos, acquires by some means or other a certain amount of olive oil, soap, silk or wax then sells the product and makes a profit, he must then lend the money to earn interest; this is the only way that profit can make more profit. And this is how it comes about that one coin attracts another, the money is nurtured in the dark and grows like the silkworm. The money-lender is always left with a profit, never a loss, unless of course he happens to be killed while carrying cash and the money falls in the dust and disappears. Even then the loss is minimal compared with the profit that comes to the household at the end of each week or month from the money that passes through the hands of strangers, the money that is loaned on interest and multiplies perpetually.

Grigoris left the graveyard because it was hot and the place smelled like honey and like a dead dog decaying in the sun after it has been poisoned or shot. He walked slowly through the village streets but he did not go past either their own house or Zervos'. At the edge of the village he urged his mind to go faster along the main road and he reached the slope of the vineyard a little before noon. His head became warmer then and into his mind crawled three lizards and a field hedgehog who hurt him, because even a hedgehog of the mind has spines which can cut into a man's flesh. After that he shortened greatly the distance between the steep track and the harvested field in front of the vineyard, and in no time at all he was standing over the spot where Zervos had fallen. Had he shortened the road a little more and brought the days closer together, he would have found Zervos still alive. But as is usual in such cases, Zervos was impatient to get his money back and hurried before daybreak to find Dikeos at home.

So Grigoris missed seeing either Zervos alive or his father after the murder. This was because, as the facts proved and as Dikeos himself confessed during the reconstruction ten days later, as soon as he fired and saw Zervos hovering over the vines, he had opened the door, holding the Mannlicher in one hand and a bag with some bread rusks and olives in the other, and took off in a north-easterly direction with the intention of hiding. He did however stop to lock the door and put the key under the stone as was his custom. This detail made the defendant's position somewhat worse. As the head of the detachment who arrested him observed shrewdly, instead of taking steps to protect his house by locking it and hiding the key, Dikeos should have tried to give assistance to his victim. Grigoris remembered afterwards that Dikeos gave a very vague reply and seemed somewhat reluctant to justify his action. But during the trial, months later, the public prosecutor referred to this detail again, and tried to support a charge of premeditated murder - which was of course what the prosecution was aiming at. The jury, however, did not give this point serious consideration when returning their verdict. They obviously interpreted it as a natural reaction, because after the deed a murderer really wishes only to protect himself and his possessions. This wish, after all, is the cause of most murders.

As he sat on his father's bed, Grigoris flew once more out of the little window, like the bullet from the Mannlicher. The difference was that this time he did not go straight ahead or upwards, but down to the time when his grandfather old Grigoris was alive, and his father was away in mainland Greece; this was between January 1914 and March 1916. It was a time when the harvest, the grape gathering, the carob-picking and all field work was still done by hand, though it felt as if it was done in the mind. And because his grandfather was able to make the day or the night either longer or shorter, there was always time left over for Grigoris to sleep, not only in his bed but also while he was eating and working. But when the old man fell off their big carob tree far up at the second waterfall of the river, the daily fluctuations of time stopped. Sometimes though, when the days grew very long and the nights short or vice versa, when a man's body grew tired and could not bear the long duration of time, Grigoris would climb as far as the waterfall by the carob tree and sit at its roots on the black rock where his grandfather had fallen and got stuck. From there he would follow the water's flow sometimes on foot but mostly inside his mind, and he would descend the waterfalls one by one as far down as the little valley behind the village.

This river, which started off with a great quantity of cold water but lost it on the way, was peculiar in that if you walked in it on foot you saw five waterfalls: two large ones and three small ones. Starting from the foot of the mountain, the second and fourth were the large ones. But if you followed the stream inside your mind, you discovered that the waterfalls were twice as many; and if you took your time, they were three times as many, though the second and fourth were always the largest.

When Grigoris, who loved the river, found Zervos on the morning of the murder lying on the ground in front of the little house in the vineyard, he was completely taken by surprise. Before running back to the village and notifying the family, he quickly took refuge for a few minutes in the river, not only because he could think calmly in its coolness, but mainly because the sight of a bloody and dusty corpse brings to mind clear and abundant waters. So he asked himself silently but specifically, what would happen now to Zervos and to all that mud and blood. And as if the river were his grandfather, Grigoris addressed himself to all categories of waters, just and unjust, sacred and profane, mineral, sulphurous and purifying: How will Zervos be cleaned and washed, Zervos the Soap-maker, who manufactures and sells soap, Zervos the Silk-winder who owns the wheel for making silken thread, Zervos the Candle-maker, who collects honeycombs and makes wax? The answer came back, again silent and specific: Let us wash him with his soap, dress him in his silk and make the sign of the cross on his feet, hands and mouth with his candles. At that point Grigoris set off limping towards the village.

Seven days after the murder, exhausted and having had no sleep for four or five days and nights, Grigoris found himself again between the big waterfall with the carob tree and the house in the vineyard. He suddenly realised that he couldn't tell what day or hour it was as he was walking aimlessly in the heat. Then, in order to avoid falling into the great chasm that has no beginning or middle, where the wind blows neither from east nor west but rushes downwards and where, as old Grigoris used to say, heavenly and earthly things mingle, Grigoris achieved with his mind as well as with his hands what is known as the technical welding-together of time. That is to say, when a man is upset by some event and the flow of his blood is altered (being that which measures and regulates time), he has a duty to himself to abandon the present, confused and unreliable as it is, and grasp a new lead, either in the past or in the future. From there he can eventually weld together the two parts of time and return safe and sound to the present. This welding occurs mostly in the mind, of course, but there are cases when one can weld time together with one's hands. So it happened that, when Grigoris put his hand in the inside pocket of his waistcoat and felt the empty cartridge from the Mannlicher and Zervos' money, time was restored to normality and at once he found himself sitting at a familiar spot, protected both from the midday heat and from the bottomless chasm of time.

Now Grigoris realised that cartridges and coins feel different to the touch not because of their shape but because of the heat of the metals. A cartridge is warm, while coins are cold. It begins as a simple piece of brass, but when it goes through the casting and charging process, that common metal acquires properties that make it unique. According to those who have worked in such factories, the bronze is first washed and cleaned thoroughly of any foreign impurities. Then it is heated to a high temperature so that it becomes dense yet at the same time light. At this stage it is as soft and pliable as dough. Then it is pressed into various moulds and shapes and, through the skill of men as well as the steady repetition of machines, the baskets fill up in no time with the finished cartridges. This is the reason why, no matter how much the cartridge cools, it always retains a temperature of its own, which affects all its parts. The lead bullet is coated with many layers of pure and tested steel (as is the case with Mannlicher bullets), so that it pierces the human body easily and disappears without trace. If one polishes and lightly oils the bullet, as Dikeos always did, the original heat of the cartridge remains undiminished and the success of a shot is guaranteed. It is also said that if the bullet kills a human being, then the cartridge takes on a reddish colour, but Grigoris had never chanced to see this phenomenon in all the years he had been collecting cartridges.

By contrast the metal of coins, whether gold, silver or copper, remains cold from the time of their making. This is probably due largely to the various devices on them, since these are almost always the severed heads of various deities, kings, governors or animals. It may be that the representation of these decapitated creatures creates the coldness; or perhaps it is certain techniques which are used in minting and subsequently in the circulation of money. Still, Grigoris looked carefully at the king with his twirled moustache and half-closed eyes, the ancient goddess of cereals and the night owl (which is said to have peculiar sleeping habits), but he could not reach any explanation for this phenomenon.

On the contrary, as he was engrossed inside the charging and cartridge-making factories, he lost the sense of direct time, the time which runs horizontally and brings the hours and the seasons, and his welding broke. Grigoris realised once again the shattering effect of the murder upon him. He was unable to chase the events away, make them go far behind the house and over the mountain, and he couldn't go to sleep. So he took the cartridge from the Mannlicher in his hands again, together with Zervos' coins, and some time between Wednesday 8th August and the following Tuesday, eve of the Dormition, he set off, walking both on foot and inside his mind, to inform the dead man's family. In his attempt not to lose sight of the fallen man, Grigoris did not walk in the normal way facing forwards but moved stepping backwards. That was why he tripped over the tall wild-rose bushes and when he reached the slope of the main road he very nearly stepped on three flying lizards, those strange, aged lizards, who, they say, are born old and die young. He did not meet a hedgehog, but seeing Zervos' head on the vines may have confused him.

On the main road he halted, unsure where to go. For a moment he thought of turning not left towards the village but right towards Chora, as he had all that money in his hands. He would cross two mountains and the big valley with the vines and the harvested grain, and the four rivers which are murky and have no waterfalls or carob trees. He would see the hill with the church of The Crucified Christ and the little chapel of

Doubting Thomas where Thomas is shown placing his fingers on the stigmata in order to believe. Then he would cross the hill with the cypress trees and enter the town. But this would require at least six hours, the vines would remain unpicked and Zervos would still be on the ground. So he turned left on the familiar road to the village and after rounding the seven bends and crossing the bridges over the three torrent beds, he reached the dead man's house out of breath. The time was eleven in the morning and Grigoris saw Markos, Zervos' elder son, sitting on the doorstep eating watermelon and spitting the pips on the ground.

Flushed though he was from running and agitated by the news he was carrying, Grigoris noticed with surprise the house flies buzzing all around Markos. The strange thing was that Grigoris was able to recall this scene much later, precisely three whole years and as many months later, when he saw Markos holding the blood-stained knife and disappearing down the river. He probably made this connection because he received the first stab of the knife whilst sitting on the black rock under the carob tree where his grandfather had been killed. He had been trying to pick out among the tree branches that little black fly which had taken the old man up in its legs, raised him high and then let him drop and crash on the rock. He was intrigued and wondered what it was that prompted this powerful fly to lift old Grigoris to the top of the tree, push him over head-first, and then allow itself to die shortly afterwards. For Grigoris remembered well how, when they brought his grandfather to the village on the back of the donkey and placed him in the big room of the house, they found a dead black fly inside his hairy nostrils: lifeless, small, with strong golden wings like the wine fly.

As for Markos, he was sitting peacefully, obviously

24

resting after working in his fields, since it was not the time of year for soap-making and the silkworms were not ready for spreading on the frames. And as far as wax-making was concerned, Grigoris knew that Markos was not interested, because this job demands a certain amount of skill. The fact that Markos usually went about without a cummerbund and unkempt showed that by nature he sought those jobs that are done from the hands outwards (jobs like digging or ploughing) and avoided those that are done from the hands inwards (like candle-making or the preparation of soap). It was said that he acquired the habit of not wearing a cummerbund when he was a baby, because his mother Irini didn't know how to swaddle a child or to put it in the customary and proper position in its cot. His mother, on the other hand, maintained that the reason why Markos was so broad and refused to wear a cummerbund was because he took after her father, Eftychios Labrinakis. Anyway, when Zervos' second son, Eftychis, was born three years after the first, Irini used to swaddle him very tightly, just to be on the safe side. So Eftychis grew up lean, white-skinned and rather thin. But after his brother stabbed the son of the murderer Dikeos in November 1931, Eftychis began to grow fat, perhaps because they continued to cook the same amount of food at home, regardless of the fact that Markos was a fugitive, and someone had to eat the left-overs.

In May 1935 Markos, still on the run, came down to the village and surrendered to the police, seeing that the political situation had changed. He was twenty four years old then, with a wife in the mountains and a year-old boy who was still unchristened. Eftychis was serving in the police force at the time; he was a cadet and had grown even fatter and whiter, while Markos had become thin and black. It was then that a strange coincidence happened, something almost unbelievable. Grigoris never knew of it, of course, being dead, but the facts are indisputable. The story goes that Markos went and gave himself up to the police because the new government had, for political reasons, granted immunity to criminal fugitives. Now Eftychis happened to be in the detachment that arrested his brother. Although he had changed in many ways, Markos still wore no cummerbund; indeed, his trousers were nearly falling down, he was so thin. Eftychis recognised the fugitive immediately, but Markos found it very difficult to believe that he had fallen into the hands of his own brother. In any case, after Markos was formally granted pardon and returned to his village, he began to recover his former shape; and when four months later he christened his son Manolis, he was already noticeably fatter.

But now Markos was still a boy, seventeen years old, and had no inkling of what was to happen in the years to come. Nor did he know, naturally, what had taken place some hours earlier, as his father was walking through Dikeos' vineyard. Grigoris too thought it would be better if such news as he was bearing was first heard by the dead man's wife, and only afterwards by the rest. So he asked Markos where his mother was, Irini 'the tall one' as she was called, not because she was actually tall, but because she considered herself to be so.

Indeed, when Irini, who was Zervos' second wife, came as a bride from another village, she said that everyone in her family was tall and that the same was true of most people in her village. Naturally this made an impression, since neither Irini nor any of those accompanying her were tall; on the contrary, an unbiased judge would claim the exact opposite. At Zervos' second wedding Grigoris was nine years old and he remembered going to church together with the groom's two daughters by his first marriage: Georgia the older one, and Agapi. They had also gone together to the funeral of their mother, the first Irini, who had bled to death in 1908. Grigoris was then seven years old, Georgia six and Agapi four. In fact, as the dead woman was being carried through the gate of the new graveyard, some blood dripped from the coffin because, apparently, Irini kept bleeding even after death. When the funeral was over, Grigoris and Zervos' girls chased each other around the yard. Grigoris was fast enough to catch little Agapi but not Georgia, who used to call him a cripple, because he was one.

When Grigoris asked Markos for his mother, he replied that she was inside making dough, his sisters were feeding the silkworms and Eftychis was either looking after the chickens or catching crabs in the river. As for his father, he may be either in the vineyards or the fields or at their beehives, or he may have fallen asleep somewhere. To this last piece of information Grigoris could have countered that Zervos was neither in the fields nor the vineyards nor at his beehives, nor asleep, because he was lying face down on the dirt-track in Dikeos' vineyard, his entrails on the ground and his head on the vines. That was where he was, and where they would find him, lying in the sun and the dust. But he preferred to remain silent, because he realised that he was too tired, especially after so many sleepless days, to give all the information that Markos would want to know. Therefore he retreated. While remaining standing on the same spot, he retreated back to his own vineyard, seating himself on his father's bed as he hoped for some sleep on the eve of the Dormition.

Not having slept since Wednesday, the day of the murder, Grigoris attributed the above event, like all the others, to the effect of the killing and the changes it

27

causes, as well as to the difficulties faced by one who changes home and bed. As it was, he had taken part in the wake for Zervos on the night of the murder, and the following night, when it became known that Dikeos had done it, Grigoris came to the big carob tree on the second waterfall, climbed the tree from which the old man had fallen and crashed onto the rock, and from there he studied all the constellations of the universe, the so-called visible and invisible world. On the nights of Friday, Saturday, Sunday and Monday 13th, while his father was still a fugitive, Grigoris went and lay on Dikeos' bed, and he may have slept for a few hours. But according to his own criteria, real sleep was something that never entered his body at all during these days. He even believed implicitly that for a week he had been in the state of what is called sleep outside the eyes or, as it is otherwise known, the sleep of oxen.

The bovine manner of sleep, while being normal and in the natural order of things for animals, is dangerous and sometimes fatal to man. Man closes his eyes and seems to fall asleep, but his sleep is outside his eyes. In this state he can hear, smell and see very clearly all around him; even through houses, trees, the ground and his own body; he can hear every sound and noise, not only loud ones but even the steps of geckos, or the growth of leaves, or the sounds of ruminating silkworms.

Above all Grigoris could hear clearly the ruminating of the silkworms when he sat up all night during Zervos' wake, while Agapi went in and out of the next room to feed them. But Grigoris did not like silkworms. No doubt their larvae produce silken thread which in turn produces capital, but they creep greedily over the mulberry branches or on the frames and they are wizened like lizards. It is also said that if a man lies on top of a silkworm frame and falls asleep, the worm possesses both the strength and greed to devour him. The darkness probably helps in this, for it is well known that silkworms love the dark just as they hate noise and the male sex. The larvae, which are all female and which give birth and do the weaving, are aware of the person who feeds them. If they do not hear the rustle of a dress and sense the smell of woman, they raise themselves up, come out of the frames and their breeding room, fall upon the green of the earth and devour men and beasts alike. But when a woman, preferably barefooted so as not to make any noise like, for instance, Agapi, comes into the dark room and feeds and tends the larvae, they not only become calm and tame but fall asleep and in their sleep they feed and grow. So it was that on the day Dikeos was arrested at the farthest carob trees (which he had claimed as his since his discharge from the army) Agapi's silkworms had fallen asleep for the fourth and last time.

This is the moment when the larva stops creeping about and acquires a glassy appearance: a sort of glass fruit on top of the dried up mulberry leaves. As she sleeps the silkworm's sleep, in the calm and the darkness, she begins to search for one end of her silken gut and unravels it from the inside outwards. And if the silkworm is well fed (something that Agapi was seeing to with great zeal), then she makes a cross of silken threads around her body and resembles a shrouded corpse. Yet the silkworm is more skilful and more persistent than those who dress the dead. What's more important, she never hurries, never fusses, never mourns. Whatever she is doing, she directs it towards herself, and her only preoccupation is how to make herself prettier. Three days pass while she weaves the silk, wrapping it round her body, and she secretes a golden thread, either from her mouth or, for reasons of natural harmony, from her tail. However, it is not known (and Grigoris was very curious to learn) whether or not the silk can be woven within the worm itself, oozing out of its mind as well.

At this point Grigoris brought himself back in front of Zervos' house and asked Markos again where his mother Irini was. He then became aware of a fact that he had not noticed all these years – Zervos had married two women with the same christian name: Irini the first, née Dikaiaki, from Dikeos' family, and Irini the tall one. Still, this did not seem unnatural to him or even strange, because he figured that men always want to find that which they have lost. So because Zervos had lost his first wife and was used to the name Irini, a head and a body called Irini, it was hard for him to change now. Grigoris even thought (leaning against the bars of the little window) that if he were to get married himself and his wife died at childbirth or bled to death, and if he were to remarry, he would choose a wife with the same name as the first. But with tall Irini suddenly appearing in the yard, her hands and apron covered in flour, Grigoris forgot all about second marriages, and if the woman had not asked him what he wanted he might have forgotten the reason for his visit, too.

Irini thus heard that her husband was lying face down in the midday sun and the dust, and she was very perplexed, not so much by Grigoris' muddled and disconnected words, as by the fact that normally at this time of day Zervos should have been at their fields, not sleeping in other people's vineyards. Then Grigoris had to become more specific and it seems that he gave a new and more detailed description of Zervos' state: his head on the vines, his mouth foaming, the black fly and the loosened cummerbund soaked in blood and bile. Although Irini understood exactly what had happened, strangely enough she did not refer at all to the substance of the matter, but said that what Grigoris was saying was

30

nonsense and not true because in eight days, next Wednesday, it is the feast of the Dormition, when fasting and mourning ceases, which means that corpses and tears are out of place. What's more, Zervos is now the church warden, and it is his job to make all the candles. He buys up all the honeycombs in the region and extracts the wax himself, a pure wax that fills the house with its smell as he pours it into clay bowls and then dips the wicks into it. It was her husband who had consecrated the little chapel of St. Marina beside Grigoris' carob tree, high up on the second waterfall, by circling it with wax. He did the same for St. Paraskevi in the valley. Also, Zervos' candles may not be white and top quality, but they are straight and thicker than those sold in the shops, that's why they burn more slowly. And who is it who melts down the remains of the big festive candles and the little yellow or white ones and recycles them? Zervos.

This argument - about melting down the burnt candles and dipping new ones, about the thrift of Zervos as warden, who saw to it that the candles were not allowed to burn for too long, saving the leftovers and repeating the cycle with no waste and with a clear profit for the church - Irini kept repeating for three days, that is, Wednesday, Thursday and Friday. Occasionally she would add details about the festivals of saints and the consecrating with wax of the twice sacred church of St. George and St. Demetrios, the little churches on the second waterfall and down in the valley and in the whole region, the whole country and the universe, both visible and invisible. On Saturday August 11th, Markos woke up earlier than usual, came out to the yard unwashed, beltless and barefoot and said aloud for all to hear - his mother, his sisters, his brother, the neighbours and the whole village from one cemetery to the other as far as

31

Dikeos' vineyard - that, if he does not find and kill the murderer, he will kill his son, the cripple, the one who is hiding in the rivers and the vineyards and is too scared to come back and sleep in his village. But Grigoris did not hear this threat until midday Wednesday 15th August, on the day of the feast of the Dormition, when he woke up from his long sleep. He did not worry, however, nor did he take any real precautions, although he avoided coming to the village. This indifference on the part of Grigoris and his neglect to take any measures for his safety were due not only to the fact that Dikeos had not yet been found and therefore Markos still had a choice, but even after the murderer had been arrested and sentenced and put in prison, Grigoris believed that he was not in any danger from Markos. And in any case, the fulfilment of such a direct and terrible threat should take at least twenty seven years.

Dikeos was sentenced to fourteen years' imprisonment because at the trial there was some confusion as to the motive of the killing. But in the second year of his sentence he died at the age of fifty three from copper disease. When the news reached the village in June 1930, Grigoris was at their vineyard clearing the dead weeds, but neither he nor anyone else in the whole area knew anything about this disease, until the day when an itinerant pedlar (who also bought honeycombs at a considerably higher price than Zervos) came to the vineyard and explained it all to Dikeos' son. The pedlar introduced himself to Grigoris as an acquaintance and fellow-prisoner of Dikeos, who had been held for political reasons under the provisions of the 1929 Special Law, passed by the strong Venizelos government of 1928. But Grigoris was impatient to hear about his father's death on that first visit of the pedlar, and he did not pay much attention either to the laws of Venizelos or to the

32

sufferings of his visitor, who had recently been released from prison. So he only took in the information that interested him, although the pedlar's story was at once a blend of political theory and an explanation of Dikeos' death. He said that when many people who are not acquainted or related to each other are put together in a confined space, like a prison, they usually develop copper disease, which is also called metal thirst. This is because men who have lived with the tools of their trade or of their household, such as hoes, sickles, ploughshares, bill-hooks, cutlery or rifles, get used to metal. In prison everything is made of wood or clay and a man, in this case Dikeos, has nothing metallic near him. What's more, Dikeos had a habit since leaving the army of sleeping on the pure metal of the Mannlicher and its polished bullets, and this made his a more extreme case. The prisoner turned green and yellow, like copper when it begins to rust; his flesh became dry, full of fibres; the inside of his body disintegrated and became completely dehydrated, before he finally died. Grigoris asked the pedlar if this disease can be developed by a prisoner who carries a coin of gold, silver or copper, but the reply he got was so complicated and unclear that in the end he failed to understand whether it was positive or negative.

The situation around Zervos' body by noon on Wednesday, the day of the murder, was just as complicated, though less unclear. Irini the tall one, Markos, his younger sister Agapi, most of the neighbours, quite a few relatives, perhaps the greater part of the village, people from the two farms in the valley and fourteen tall men from Irini's village, plus Grigoris - all gathered round Zervos, some having walked there, others having made this journey inside their minds. Eftychis was wading in the river, engrossed in catching crabs, and did not hear the news until three hours later, when

33

he returned home and found his father laid out in the middle of the big room next to the silkworms' room. As for Georgia, who didn't like walking about in the streets, she refused to come out into the heat and stayed behind to prepare the house. Grigoris arrived last at the vineyard, due to his lameness. He counted the people there both mentally and with his finger and calculated that if they did not lift the dead man soon, part of the vineyard was sure to be destroyed, as most of the spectators were stepping carelessly in and out of the vines. But presently many people began to leave and return to their work not only because of the heat but because Irini was wailing loudly - endlessly counting candles, the donations of candles, and the consecrating of churches with wax. She kept saying how the takings of the church treasury had increased during the months of her husband's wardenship, that is from January to August. Finally, the case of Zervos confirmed the fact that a gunshot ceases to arouse interest after awhile, whereas questions build up as to the murderer and the reasons for the murder.

Having been notified of the event, the authorities sent a detachment from the nearest town, the capital of the province, made up of three policemen and a sergeant, to carry out an investigation on the spot and clarify the matter. The policemen arrived at the scene of the crime early in the afternoon, when Zervos had been laid out in the coolness of his own house. They examined the whole area, made note of the blood on the ground and banned everyone from passing through before the investigation had been completed. After that, they measured various distances radially, using as the centre either Zervos' blood or Dikeos' little house. They went up on the roof of the house, climbed on all the trees in the vineyard and, crawling and leaping, reached the harvested field and the fence with the wild roses and then came as far as the slope that leads to the road. Two hours later the sergeant announced that Zervos had been shot from the fence as he was going past the track of the vineyard, heading towards the village. He only happened to fall in the direction of the house, because when someone is shot in the stomach he usually spins round on the spot one hundred and eighty degrees, that is he turns to face the other way. But if the man who is shot is strong, the angle can be three hundred and sixty degrees. Therefore, because the traces on the ground showed that Zervos had fallen a little to the right, had turned, that is, by three quarters of a circle, the sergeant concluded that the deceased was of great strength. This conclusion added considerable authority to the man heading the detachment, because the deceased was indeed of great strength. He had married twice and fathered many children, four living and three dead, within eight years (from 1916 when he was discharged from Venizelos' civil guard, to 1924); he had extended his house twice, worked in the fields and his four vineyards, manufactured soap, wax and silk and was, by general consent, the best builder of charcoal or lime kilns. The making of soap and silk had eventually been taken over by his daughters, the vineyards and fields by his sons, and Irini the tall one dipped the candles more carefully and thinly than her husband. Zervos himself only built kilns now and was very active on the church council.

But what Zervos was really good at was investing his capital, that is the cash which a man can carry and lend on interest, secretly or openly; secondly, he was a very important official in the local Liberal party, which governed the country at that time. In the little house in the vineyard, Grigoris asked himself again whether Zervos' murder and the imminent elections of the

35

following Sunday 19th August, were in some way connected, but he could not reach any definite conclusion. After all, both the murderer and the victim belonged to the same political party, although of course Dikeos did not have the active patronage of Zervos. Moreover, no political gain could justify the murder, since the popularity of the Liberal party was so great that no power seemed strong enough to hold it back.

Which is exactly what Dikeos himself maintained immediately after his arrest. Two days before the elections, on 17th August to be precise, after the ninth-day memorial service had been conducted for the dead man, a villager had informed the sergeant (who had been sent some days before to investigate and was at the village again to maintain law and order during the elections) that the murderer was hiding in a hut on the left side of the mountain, near the disputed carob trees. Although similar information had turned out to be false in the past and the same hut had been searched as well as that whole area, the sergeant could not ignore the informant, and circled Dikeos' hideout with his detachment two hours before dawn on Saturday 18th August. One hour later the wanted man came out of the hut, unarmed, and loosened his cummerbund in order to relieve himself. Dikeos was arrested without resistance and led straight to the vineyard for a reconstruction. Because the air was heavily charged with the political climate of that day, it was natural that the sergeant (who was a Peloponnesian by origin) should ask Dikeos whether his action had any political motives. Somewhat taken aback by the question, Dikeos replied negatively. He gave the same reply, this time with some irritation (noted by Grigoris who was present and knew his father's temperament), when he was asked if he had searched the dead man for money. He did explain, though, that he

36

knew, just as every villager knew, that Zervos used to carry money on him even when working in the fields, but he said he did not kill for money; that such an idea had never crossed his mind and that the shooting was accidental and he may have done it in his sleep, when he had heard someone approach the house.

Such persistence on Dikeos' part, coupled with the absence of any corroborative evidence as to the direction that Zervos was heading when he was shot, convinced the sergeant even more that the shot had been fired from the fence and not from the window of the little house. Dikeos, on the other hand, stated that Zervos was coming toward the house, which is why he fell in that direction; that the bullets of a Mannlicher are humane; that he fired in his sleep without seeing who the man was, and so on and so forth. But since no one questioned him about loans and interest rates, Dikeos had no reason to refer to these matters. After all, Zervos always lent money secretly, and always on interest. Grigoris too remained silent when questioned about money and the missing cartridge. In the presence of his father he replied negatively, just as he had done during the previous two interrogations. The sergeant was particularly insistent on the subject of the cartridge; during the reconstruction the suggestion was raised that every single vine be searched, both the raisin and the sultana vines, which had since been harvested. However after careful consideration the sergeant abandoned his plan and considered the matter of the cartridge closed, secretly fearing that if the cartridge was found on the left or the right side of the road, it would be hard to explain the about-turn of Zervos before he fell. The argument concerning the great strength of the deceased might then be undermined; so the sergeant decided not to put the original police report in jeopardy but to state for the second and last time, on the additional evidence of the reconstruction, that Zervos had been shot from the fence, head-on.

Grigoris of course had a different opinion, agreeing with his father. Yet on Wednesday, the day of the murder, he was not aware of this detail, since the murderer was still unknown. What he did notice that day was that he went to the vineyard and back to the village five times, each time on foot. On the night of the wake, sitting next to the silkworms and facing Agapi, he went to their vineyard another fifteen times, though only inside his mind. But at midday and in the afternoon he actually walked there every time. The first time was when he found Zervos drowned in his blood and his stomach acids, motionless among the restless flies. The next time he was with Zervos' wife, with Markos, Agapi and thirty eight others, but not Eftychis and Georgia. Eftychis was catching crabs in the river and did not come to the vineyard then. Georgia was in the house when Grigoris brought the news about her father, but she refused to come out because she was ashamed of walking with a limp.

The reason why Zervos' elder daughter was lame was that in September 1922, when she was twenty years old, the soap vat had fallen on her. It was after the Asia Minor disaster, when six refugee families had arrived at the village together with the soldiers who had survived and returned home. At that time all prices went up because the currency was devalued by half and production was noticeably lower. The price of soap reached thirty lepta per bar and in the haste to prepare it the vat tilted over and fell on Georgia's right foot. Georgia had caught the vat in time, so no worse damage occurred, but by the time they had run and freed her foot, the injury had been done. Afterwards there was an argument amongst the three village practitioners as to whether they should place the injured foot in plaster or in a splint or wrap it in gauze and sheep's wool. In the end they agreed to combine all three methods and try out the new technique on the damaged foot. After three months Georgia was able to walk, but she had been left lame. She was now ashamed of coming out into the street limping, for she was used to running and walking only on foot since childhood, and she didn't know how to walk inside her mind.

Grigoris left the crowd that had gathered in their vineyard and went to fetch their donkey to carry the dead man, since no one else thought of it; if Zervos was left there all day this would mean incalculable consequences for both the vineyard and himself. So when he came back to the little house for the fourth time, in the afternoon, together with the detachment, Zervos' two sons and four or five of his relatives, the place had been cleared and was quiet. Eftychis was barefoot and in a great hurry to see the spot where his father had been found, but the sergeant called out to him to wait and not disturb the footprints. Eftychis, who was to become a policeman several years later, obeyed and slowed his pace. The mention of footprints puzzled Grigoris, since so many people had walked up and down and trodden over a large area of the vineyard, but he preferred to remain silent in front of a representative of the government. His father (who had served in the police force before the Great Division and knew all about these things) often used to say that only one who is in the wrong should speak to a policeman or army officer. This is because the wrong-doer may of course worsen his position, but he is already in trouble. Whereas an innocent man will never find justice if he starts chatting to a policeman; but he can answer with a simple yes or no, only when he is asked. Those who have nothing to do with the case but happen to be present, should always remain silent in front of the authorities, displaying no emotion and taking no sides. Nevertheless, as Grigoris discovered a few days later at the reconstruction, his father did not follow this policy faithfully because, although he was in the wrong having committed a murder, he did not talk as much as he should have, but confined himself to basics.

The last time Grigoris came to their vineyard on the day of the murder was at eight o'clock in the evening. There was still light in the sky and on the ground, although the sun had disappeared behind the western hills. At the slope just before the wild roses Dikeos' son paused and there the coolness of the mountain reached him. He sat on a stone and gazed due south. He could see the village, two or three hills, the valley, and in the distance the long mountain range which was a boundary for the region and formed the funnel of the world. Grigoris could race through this funnel from top to bottom, round and round, always inside his mind. It would never have been possible for him to circle the mountains on foot, starting from the bottom and winding up to the top. Even if he could, how would he be able to leave the ridges and walk in the air, gyrating as far as the heavenly dome? He was indeed able to climb to a great height with his eyes but, as his grandfather had explained to him, the eye can only see what is visible, and you need bright light and strong eyesight. That is why the smoothest way is the way of the imagination, which travels slowly but surely and in depth. This manner is also called the way of the silken ladder and he who follows it hangs from it like a spider. He scrambles up to the heavenly dome and strolls around the seven constellations and the bounteous waters of the Galaxy.

Since Zervos was the only man in the village who had the means to weave a silken ladder (which had to be of a specific height and width) Grigoris had asked his grandfather, with the indiscretion and naivety of a child, whether the Silk-winder had more chances than anyone else of climbing to the heavenly dome. The old man's reply was quite different from what Grigoris expected. He gave an answer all right, but it was neither a straightforward reply to the question nor an allegorical one - which puzzled Grigoris greatly. Now, sitting on the warm stone on the slope of the vineyard, with some lingering lizards still running around beside him at a height of one metre, he calculated that in order for someone to produce a silken ladder leading up to the first constellation, he would need Zervos' lifetime twice or three times over, thousands of mulberry trees with wide leaves to feed the silkworms in not just one room but at least fifty or sixty, and just as many women headed by Agapi to look after them and lull them to sleep. However, such an operation could bring enormous profits and considerable capital, so it was doubtful whether they would use so much fine silk just to weave silken ladders.

Contemplating all this, Grigoris walked past the fence with the wild roses and entered the track through the vineyard without meeting anyone, alive or dead. There, at the precise moment when he was picking up the key from underneath the stone, he began to wonder for the first time about his father's absence and the locked-up house. At that same moment, high up in the mountain beside the disputed carob trees, Dikeos was preparing to spend his first night as a fugitive away from the vineyard where he had been sleeping for eight consecutive years since 1920, after his beehives were destroyed. In those days they owned thirteen beehives on the barren hill behind the vineyard. In a good year Dikeos would extract a hundred to a hundred and five okas of honey, which he sold to Zervos, together with the honeycombs, at the current price. Zervos stored the honey, as he did the oil, the wine, the carobs and the raisins, and when the respective price went up he would load the produce and resell it in Chora. But one morning that year, in the month of October (shortly before the honey is harvested), when Venizelos had lost the elections, Dikeos had found all his bees dead. Someone had for some unknown reason blocked the entrances to the beehives with mud and the bees had died. Dikeos discovered this after three days; he took the lids off the beehives, collected the dead bees, scraped up the remaining honey and sold it to Zervos at a very low price, setting it against what he owed. Then he broke up and burnt the beehives. He collected his clothes in the middle of the night from the house in the village, wrapped the Mannlicher in a blanket and installed himself in the little house in the vineyard. From then on he stopped speaking loudly, as he had been taught in the army, and started speaking softly. However, it is probable that he used to speak loudly even before he joined the civil guards and possibly from the time he married Maria the Quiet One, who died at childbirth when only nineteen. Then again, he may have cried loudly as an infant or even as a baby inside his mother's belly. For this is the beginning of man's nature, when he is not yet born. One person may be born and live his life on the side of speech, while another on the side of listening. It is therefore very serious if someone changes one of his natural habits and it is regarded as though he has broken away from his origins and is alone in the world, without father or mother, without friends or relatives, like the lone field hedgehog who curls up deep within itself, its spines showing on the outside.

Grigoris returned to the village as the first stars were lighting up, the ones that his grandfather called 'cockerels' because they were like the dawn cocks. Later, as he sat in Zervos' big room taking part in the wake while Agapi fed the silkworms in the next room, he went to and from their vineyard countless times. In between he also went to the big carob tree high up on the second waterfall where his grandfather was killed, but he didn't stop. He flowed down with the river and once he even went far south past the valley and began to climb the mountains. On the ridge he halted, lost in thought and exhausted. He looked deep into the night at the sea below and far in the distance, without however attempting a descent. He was afraid lest the sea enter his brain, the naked sea being an intangible and unpredictable element. He might drown just then, alone on the dark beach, far away from Zervos' corpse and Agapi. And it was indeed Agapi who came into the room again and by speaking to him brought him back home. Before falling asleep in the chair, Grigoris had just enough time to go to their vineyard once more, and then he thought he saw his father sitting on the doorstep, his boots and socks off, cooling his feet.

Then Dikeos' son prepared to return to the house when something else caught his attention. He thought he saw from Zervos' room his father, sitting bareheaded and calm, holding on his knees the Mannlicher, clean and shiny, in the position of a sleeping child. He thought Dikeos was saying something which could not be heard in the room where the dead man was, due to the distance as well as the persistent ruminating of the silkworms. Grigoris felt sorry that his father had given up the habit of shouting loudly, and silently asked him to repeat what he had said. But Dikeos did not comply with his

43

son's request, perhaps because he was afraid of disturbing the silkworms or of waking up the sleeping rifle. He appeared to retreat into the darkness of the night, leaving the Mannlicher naked on the cool doorstep. Then Grigoris felt great terror, because he knew from his grandfather that a rifle, especially a Mannlicher, must either be held in the hands or wrapped up in a blanket and nursed with care. He knew that years ago they used to have a front-loading rifle at home but it got lost, because rifles find their own way and choose the house they want to live in. Also, that the Mannlicher came to their house one morning wrapped in an army blanket and that if it were ever stolen it would still find its way back all by itself. This had actually happened twice in the past, when the police had requisitioned the rifle, taking advantage of a change of government; but the third time something different happened, as the facts proved afterwards: when Dikeos was arrested on the eve of the elections of 19th August, the rifle was seized and the charge of illegal possession and use of firearms was added to the charges faced by the murderer. Even so, Grigoris expected the rifle to return home, up to the day when he was stabbed, but this never happened - perhaps because it was left naked and neglected for so long, or perhaps because its masters, old Grigoris and Dikeos, were both dead.

The only thing left to Grigoris was the empty cartridge and as he was sitting half asleep on his father's bed on the eve of the Dormition, he suddenly thought that maybe this cartridge, together with all the other cartridges he had collected and kept in the house in the village, could draw the Mannlicher back home and in its turn the Mannlicher would bring Dikeos. He had been having the same thoughts during the night of the wake, but ever since Dikeos surrendered and the Mannlicher

44

left home, Grigoris began to believe that the steady attraction which exists between a cartridge, a rifle and a man had for some reason become weaker. After Dikeos' death in prison from copper disease, it became apparent that the age-old relationship between the Dikeakises and rifles had completely broken down.

This relationship had begun in the days of old Grigoris, or perhaps earlier, when necessity and the love of freedom forced the people of the region to take to the mountains. It is even said that Dikeos' own grandfather was for a time a rifle-maker and repairer of wine barrels and that one day when he was inside an open barrel cleaning it he was killed by the Turks, the infidel foreigners, who also burnt down his shop. His son, old Grigoris, took refuge in the mountains unarmed, but when nine months later he returned to the village he was carrying two new short-barrelled Italian rifles, his booty.

So in August 1910, when Venizelos won the elections in mainland Greece and formed a government of his own, Grigoris was nine years old. Then his grandfather had loaded one of the rifles and helped his grandson fire in the air to celebrate the occasion. Grigoris remembered that the rifle kicked three times in his hands for Venizelos' sake; that he then collected his first spent cartridges and he was to add to his collection at later feasts and elections. The last time he fired was November 1916, one month after the creation of the State of Thessaloniki during the minor festival of St. George the Intoxicator. It was then that they opened their barrels and his father, who had been away for two years, tried their own wine. People say it is easier to get drunk on that day because the saint also lends a hand. Dikeos had felt a strange elation, not knowing that his father was to be killed seven days later. He had taken the new Mannlicher

45

out of the chest, come out to the yard and fired three times. Grigoris had picked up three cartridges and that had made fifty seven, counting a fourth one that he had fired himself. But ever since his grandfather had fallen and had been killed by the black fly, Grigoris had stopped collecting cartridges; not only because his father took the Mannlicher to the vineyard, but because one cannot spend a whole lifetime collecting empty cartridges.

Now, with the single cartridge in his pocket, Grigoris remembered the night of the wake and asked himself whether he had really seen his father that night in Zervos' house, sitting barefoot on the doorstep, cooling himself and lulling the Mannlicher to sleep.

In reality Dikeos took his boots off only ten days later. As soon as the reconstruction was over, the prisoner told his son Grigoris to fetch him a pair of socks and the clay jug, so that he could wash and change. The sergeant granted this request, either because he considered that the prisoner was entitled to it, or because he wished to pay some sort of tribute to an old comrade-in-arms; but mainly because he was in no hurry to get back to the village and there was no danger of the murderer escaping. Dikeos unlaced his boots and then Grigoris was able to get very close to his father and take the boots off for him one by one, as he had done in the old days with his grandfather's shoes. So he saw his father's feet, white with red blisters, the socks worn at the heels. Then he poured water from the jug into Dikeos' palms and Dikeos scrubbed and dried his feet carefully, sitting on the doorstep of his house. When his father finished washing, Grigoris went behind the vines and picked some leaves from their little pomegranate tree for his father to put inside his boots to stop them sweating, just like old Grigoris used to do. Dikeos dried his feet, put on the clean socks, shook the boots to get the stones out and placed the pomegranate leaves inside them. While he was tying his laces, his son observed that Dikeos' ring was missing, and that his fingers and palms were thinner than usual. He also noticed that his eyes had become somewhat larger and all his body had taken on a different shape. Grigoris explained this phenomenon as a result of the discomforts and deprivations which the life of a fugitive brings. But he could not explain the loss of the ring, something that was to prove fatal for Dikeos, who crossed the prison gates bereft of any piece of metal on his person.

The same applied to Grigoris up until Thursday morning, the day of the victim's funeral. No coin or cartridge was on his person on the night of the wake, as he slept on the chair in short and irregular doses. Around three in the morning, the time when the constellation of the Plough disappears in the south and when the Big Ape and the Little Ape or Monkey appear in the north, Grigoris sank into an easier sleep. Agapi was still going to and fro feeding the silkworms, the big candles around the dead man were burning and gradually getting shorter and shorter, and inside the coffin the sprigs of basil and marjoram had lost their gloss and their leaves were becoming softer. Grigoris felt all these changes but he did not worry about this amazing clarity of his senses. In the past, lying asleep beside his grandfather, he could follow the old man as he got up long after midnight, opened the door, had a pee at the edge of the garden and counted the stars and the hours of the night. Of course his grandfather had been dead for twelve years and Grigoris slept alone in his bed. But even now the old man would sometimes come and shake him out of his sleep at the hour when he was supposed to get up and go to work. Perhaps the old man was allowed these excursions from the underworld because

47

he had lived longer than his daughter-in-law, Maria the Quiet One. Maria had never in those twenty seven years come up to see Grigoris and wake him up; but it is certain that she asked every villager who went down there about her son. Maybe, being so young when she died, she had forgotten the way back to the house where she had given birth to Grigoris and struggled with the family saint. But she did watch Grigoris grow up, go to work alone in the empty fields, walk the visible and invisible world on foot and in his mind; of that there is no doubt. All the newcomers brought her news, some more some less; but most of all old Grigoris, when in 1916 he went to stay with his daughter-in-law once again, in that part of the universe. On this topic, people assert categorically that every village and every town of the so-called living world corresponds to a place in the underworld. That is, there is an exact correspondence between the two realms, and each dead person has his own place awaiting him in the respective village or town of the underworld. The fact that there is a continuous influx of people descending upon that world, neither alters things nor does it pose any problems for those already there. And here lies the difference between one world and the other, as those who have some knowledge of these matters maintain. Namely, that the living world, in this case Grigoris Dikeakis' village, exists on one level only, whereas its twin village down below exists on an infinite number of levels, which are actually easily recognisable from one another, since they are supported and preserved by the thoughts of all new arrivals.

Now as far as Zervos is concerned, it is hard to say what sort of information he could offer Maria about her son. But one thing is certain: he could inform with great accuracy all those villagers who might wish to know the current price of oil, wax, silk, and generally of all agricultural products or the rate of daily wages. All these thoughts Grigoris could contain in his head easily and clearly, in-between his small doses of sleep. But then he began to hear the ruminating noises of the silkworms in the next room; he was able to watch the snakelike movement of each hungry larva and feel the first creakings coming from Zervos' prone body, together with the growing decomposition of the flowers inside the open coffin. Grigoris knew now without a doubt that his natural, human sleep was lost forever and in its place had come the dreaded sleep of the oxen.

The wake finished at six in the morning, but Grigoris had left an hour earlier. He took the main road, unwashed, unkempt, without food or drink, reached the slope and after passing through the gate with the roses he came into their vineyard. At this hour, particularly in that deserted part of the fields, the light becomes infra-red in the upper layers of the atmosphere, while down below on the ground, especially where the earth has been newly sown, it turns to violet. Anyone passing the track through the vineyard, for example Zervos or Grigoris, could have seen Dikeos' house glimmering white in the morning shadows, disappearing and reappearing again. But it is doubtful whether he could have seen the barrel of a rifle that might perhaps emerge from the little window. It would only be the bullet and the astonishment from the impact and the noise that would testify to the event. Zervos' son Eftychis was standing now on the spot where his father had fallen, examining the place after the sergeant's example. Grigoris recognised Eftychis easily, but he thought it wise to retreat to the fence and watch the goings-on without getting involved. Zervos' younger son knocked on the door of the house three times, calling out at the same time, but received no answer, something that surprised Grigoris. His surprise became even

49

greater when he went into the house after Eftychis had gone and discovered that the Mannlicher, the bullets and all the rusks and olives were gone. The tools stood undisturbed with the harvest baskets and the coil of wire for catching the hare, the weasel and the nocturnal badger. Grigoris decided that the hour had come, now that the grapes were ripe, to set wire traps along the trails through the vineyard, in order to protect their property from the animals of the field.

At that precise moment, close to sunrise, Eftychis opened the door of the big room and announced to his family (while the candles were already half consumed) that if the murderer is one of the villagers, then it must be Dikeos. But if the murderer is an outsider, then Dikeos, having heard the shot in his vineyard, must have gone after him. This explains why he hasn't appeared up to now and hasn't slept in his house in the vineyard or in the village.

Eftychis' conjecture sounded perfectly logical to all the members of Zervos' family. In fact, it gained further credence when half an hour later a cousin of the victim remembered that yesterday, Wednesday, at dawn, as he was passing opposite Dikeakis' vineyard, he heard a shot. Ten minutes later as he turned the corner and came nearer, he saw Dikeos going off towards the mountain, to the north-east. Then he remembered more clearly that Dikeos was holding his rifle, that his bootlaces were undone and that he was running as if pursued. Three months later, when Dikeos was finally sitting in the dock facing a murder charge, that same first cousin of Zervos appeared in court as a witness for the prosecution. He mentioned then all the details he had remembered in the meantime and especially insisted on describing the murderer's face, pointing out that on that morning Dikeos' expression had been that of a killer; he was smoking like a black man and his cheeks were yellow and sunken, because they say that whoever sheds another man's blood sheds his own at the same time. This explanation of Dikeos' pallor did not interest the court at all, although Zervos' lawyer used the point very skilfully. But Markos, who was present at the trial, understood the meaning of his uncle's phrase and repeated it word for word when he addressed Grigoris just before stabbing him three years later: if someone sheds another man's blood, he sheds his own at the same time. Due to the situation he found himself in at that moment, Grigoris failed to make the proper connection and to understand what Markos meant. But he did manage to remember, as he was bleeding profusely, Markos' threat some days after Zervos' death, that if he didn't kill the murderer he would kill his son, the cripple. Grigoris had fallen half in the river and half on the bank and had no use for his legs. It did however cross his mind that it wasn't quite right to say that his father's blood was also his own, apart from kinship of course. Surely every man has his very own constitution, his own bones and entrails. Similarly, he has his own angel and the black fly that lives inside him until his death. But because Grigoris' blood and entrails were already spilling into the swollen river and flowing as far as the valley, where the water disappears and reeds and swamp plants grow, the stabbed man stopped thinking about shared blood and focused on his own, stretched on his back under the big carob tree.

Now, also lying on his back on his father's bed, one week after Zervos' murder, on Tuesday at about two in the afternoon, he focused on that point in the sky which brings human sleep and rests the spirit. But their whole vineyard came between his eyes and the point of sleep. A way had to be found for picking and gathering the grapes before any further loss or damage could occur. Then the vineyard vanished, together with the tasks of picking, spreading in the sun and gathering in of the raisins. Grigoris shut his eyes, holding on to the sunlit dome of the sky with his mind only, while deep inside him he began to hear the clear voices of cicadas on the olive trees of the vineyard, then the manoeuvres of worms inside the roots of trees. Finally, the ceaseless ruminating of Agapi's silkworms was heard, coming from three kilometres away.

B

In a rocky region nine or ten kilometres north-east of
Dikeos' vineyard, right on the border between the village
and the town which was the provincial capital, there
were six or seven carob trees. Dikeos disputed the
ownership of these trees, not with any of his neighbours,
but with the local authority. Due to uncertainty as to the
exact boundaries between the two municipalities and
also the absence of any title deeds, Dikeos considered
the carob trees as his, maintaining that he had harvested
them for over twenty years and that the little nearby
stone hut had been built by his father two years before
his death, at the time when he was a volunteer on the
mainland. The forestry commissioner of the big village
had sued Dikeos three times in four years but, because
the case extended beyond the jurisdiction of the forestry
commission or the Court of Appeal at Chora, a decision
was still pending and only a final definition of the
district boundaries could put an end to the dispute
between the citizen and the state. In real terms, the
dispute ended in 1928 with the imprisonment of Dikeos,
but this only became official after 1933, when the
government changed hands and Venizelos' party was
removed from power.

During the long series of Venizelist governments the
case of the ill-defined boundaries was repeatedly looked
into by the local authorities but because the party big
wigs in both villages had roughly the same power and
the same influence over the municipal committees, the
boundaries were never properly defined, even though
officials and parliamentary candidates kept promising

in their election manifestos to settle the matter once and for all. It was at such times that this insignificant matter acquired extraordinary importance; more often than not the whole political debate and the exercise of party-political muscle centred upon Dikeos' carob trees, which, by the way, nobody else seemed to want.

Once, however, Dikeakis nearly lost the carob trees for ever. This happened after the Asia Minor disaster, when the so-called revolutionary government of 1922-24 took the decision to distribute among the refugees certain pieces of land which did not have clear title deeds, as is the case with municipal or monastic land. The municipality of the big village included in the redistribution Dikeos' carob trees, wishing on the one hand to show zeal in the matter and on the other to avoid handing out other, richer land. The day was saved by Emmanuel Zervos, who showed a genuine desire and ability to help Dikeos. At the same time, this gave him a chance to prove to the village that he had real political clout and that he didn't permit anyone to harm their community. Twice he went to see the municipal governor and so managed both to sort out his own affairs and to overturn the decision to hand over the disputed area to the refugees.

Still, even if the land had gone to the landless refugees from Asia Minor, it is certain that it would have been practically useless, because those people were said to be unaccustomed to steep mountains, they had never seen a carob tree before and, more importantly, the quantity of carobs produced each year was small and of indifferent quality. If one considers that the current price of carobs in the year Zervos was murdered was one to sixteen compared with top quality olive oil and one to thirteen compared with sultanas, it is easy to see that the disputed trees were not such an enormous loss.

What mattered was that the area remained free for Dikeos to exploit and that even a disputed property must not be lost. As Dikeos never spent any money on those carob trees (in contrast to the big tree on the second waterfall), he was left with a small and certain profit.

Now the reason why Dikeos chose the area of the carob trees to hide, instead of heading towards any other point on the horizon, is something which only he was able to explain in the fairly long series of letters he wrote to his son from prison. Yet the reasons which Dikeos put forward in great detail were of no real value to Grigoris, who would have understood his father's motives even without those letters. It seems that Dikeos wanted to hand down through the ancient practice of writing all that he had done or wanted to do and even all his thoughts during the eighteen months of his imprisonment. This is how one should explain his written account of a theory which, as Dikeos pointed out, he had conceived on his second day on the run, while he watched from his hideout as the police detachment carefully combed the area all around him. Already on Thursday afternoon, 9th August, immediately after Zervos' funeral, the detachment made a circling move towards the mountains to the north-east, passing within just fifty metres of the murderer, but saw no tracks nor any other indication that the wanted man was hiding nearby. This particular incident and all that followed helped Dikeos to express his theory better and to describe it to his son in seven letters, written on prison stationery and bearing the censor's stamp.

More specifically, Dikeos had been taught that what people usually call life is a series of incidents that begin early in the morning and, after adapting and developing according to the circumstances of the day, disappear into the falling night. So the murderer came to the conclusion that man himself is but a day-long event. He exists only for that day, from the time he wakes up and performs his morning routine to the moment when he retires to bed late at night. This day, however often it is repeated, will always follow its foreordained pattern, regardless whether man is the active cause of events or its passive victim.

Whenever Dikeos applied his mind to the events of his own life, whether active or passive in nature, his conclusion was always similar; as for example in the case of the murder, the trial and his imprisonment. Thus everything that happened took place whether he willed it or not, the only difference being whether the events were active or passive.

Dikeos considered it to be an active step in his life when he decided to leave his hideout for two hours on Thursday morning and go down to the big village, to sell his ring and purchase tobacco and food for the remaining days of hiding. He considered his hiding himself away from the world as a passive reaction which he had been forced into not only by the events which had taken place and his natural fear of the consequences but also by the very instincts inherited by man from primitive times. This was the crux of Dikeos' whole theory and it allowed him to see any events as alternately active or passive.

It is said that after a murder the perpetrator must remain hidden until the ninth day after the death of the victim, being extra careful during the first three days. Experience shows that after the middle of the third day following a natural or violent death, the dead man's family reach the climax of their grief and distress. This is the most dangerous time, when the relatives might take the law into their own hands and exact vengeance and the police ought to take strong preventative measures. The danger begins to diminish after the third day and the situation returns to normal, only to become critical again on the ninth day, after which the mourners finally despair and the great danger facing the murderer ceases. It is his turn then to come forward and give himself up to the authorities.

The third and ninth day of mourning for the dead man; the rituals that have to be observed unchanged; and most of all the meticulous care that a murderer takes in order not to provoke the victim's family during that time - it was for these reasons that Dikeos remained in the mountains rather than surrendering himself immediately to the police. It all came out during the preliminary investigation and the court hearing, Dikeos not always displaying the necessary eloquence or persuasiveness.

On both occasions the examining magistrate and the prosecution were more interested to hear why Dikeos remained hidden after the murder, rather than why he had committed the crime. They explained to him that a murder may be the act of a moment brought about in an evil hour, and that we can never know its causes because the soul is dark and unfathomable. But those passions which occasionally lead us to the heinous act of manslaughter cease to exist once the murder has been committed and therefore the murderer ought to give himself up to the authorities and accept the appropriate punishment. By doing so, he shows his repentance and possibly improves his position. In Dikeos' case it was pointed out, more than once, that he could have avoided justice for the rest of his life if the police hadn't captured him, which demonstrated his hard and violent character, as well as his hatred towards the deceased and society as a whole. On the other hand, the defendant maintained that as he was not arrested immediately after the crime, when passions were still running high, he could only give himself up after nine days had passed, on account of the family's mourning and grief. He said that he had helped the police to capture him and that he even expected to be arrested on Friday 17th August, not, as it turned out, the day after.

Dikeakis' lawyer (who had been appointed by the court due to the inability of the murderer to pay for a lawyer of his own) intervened two or three times, invoking the defendant's fear as the main cause of his flight. He ended his defence by accepting Dikeakis' guilt and pleading for leniency. The court didn't seem to pay any attention to his words, but in the end, they passed a comparatively light sentence on the defendant for reasons which were never made entirely clear. Nevertheless the lawyer of the victim's family (who had been included on the Liberal ballot sheet in the August elections two months before the hearing, and had failed to be elected as an MP) succeeded in persuading the court to award damages for mental distress amounting to fifteen thousand drachmas or its equivalent, forty gold sovereigns. To this amount were added one thousand five hundred drachmas to cover legal costs.

Grigoris, who was present at the trial, had in his waistcoat pocket one sovereign, one twenty-drachma piece and two drachmas from Zervos' money, together with the cartridge from the Mannlicher, and another five hundred drachmas in notes from the sale of twenty five okas of sultanas. He calculated in his head and with his fingers that in order to pay the sum he would have to sell the whole year's olive oil, the remaining sultanas, the largest of the black raisins and the carobs from the big tree and from the disputed trees on the mountain. Given that the greatest part of the sultanas had been destroyed by the unexpected flood of Monday 20th

August, the day after the elections, and that there remained only forty okas after selling the twenty five, Grigoris' prospects of paying this court fine seemed remote. Moreover for payment to be at all feasible, each type of produce had to be sold at the highest possible price for the next three years. But if Grigoris kept one third of the oil for his needs and if the production of sultanas and large raisins was lower than usual, then payment of the fine would take at least four years. He did not include among these products any of the barley or pulses, because they came in very small quantities and, more importantly, if he sold them he would have nothing to eat for four whole years.

These simple thoughts, coupled with the fact that payment of the sixteen thousand five hundred drachmas had to be made within a month otherwise Dikeos' property would be confiscated, forced Grigoris into action during the rest of November and the first two weeks of December. He sold all that year's produce, except for the barley and pulses. He also sold their donkey for a fairly good price, the one who had carried the dead Zervos, as well as two plots of land.

This land was bought by a family of refugees who had received a loan from the government but had to make up the required sum by selling a silver bracelet which, it was said, had survived the disaster that befell those people in their homeland. The first plot lay to the west of the village and contained thirteen olive trees, half of what the Dikeakis family owned. Of course this sale meant that the annual production of olive oil was reduced by half, down to about ninety okas, but Grigoris was hopeful that he would still cover his needs. The second plot was in the valley and it was the one that gave most of the annual barley. The purchase price for this piece of land turned out to be quite high, not because it was particularly big or fertile, but because at one end it had a stone threshing floor, built, Grigoris knew, by his great-grandfather. It stood on a small land-rise and was therefore always well aired for threshing - an important asset for those who knew how still the valley could be during the summer.

On December 10th 1928, one month after the trial, Grigoris went to the state treasury of the main village, the district capital, and paid sixteen and a half thousand drachmas. He had one hundred and forty five drachmas left after selling everything and he sent these by post to the prisoner. He had also given him another four hundred drachmas for cigarettes and other small expenses, immediately after the pronouncement of the verdict.

At this point something must be mentioned which none of the villagers noticed and which had no obvious effect on the economic life of the place, yet is still noteworthy. Even though Grigoris sent sixty to seventy drachmas each month to his father for cigarettes, he was still able to buy a quantity of barley, up until the day he was stabbed. And even though the oil production had been reduced by half, Dikeos' son lived as before, while most of Zervos' money was still in his pocket. This was at a period when the purchasing value of the drachma had already fallen by one quarter. Grigoris did not live through the national bankruptcy of 1932, during which the Venizelos government of 1928 was forced to devalue the drachma by sixty percent, but it is certain that even then, his situation would not have changed substantially in the midst of the general economic crisis faced by the Liberal bourgeois establishment.

For administering the estate and the household economy, Grigoris was following (with no special effort but with excellent results) the so-called lifestyle of the field lizard, not of the domestic silkworm as Zervos did when he was alive. According to this method, known to most of the farmers in the region and exercised studiously by old Grigoris over the sixty seven years of his life, the lizard demonstrates with clarity and persistence that the drier the soil where she lives and the more blistering the sun and the wind, the more easily she is nourished. What's more her body grows in these adverse and hostile conditions in a way completely different from all other animals. She begins life as an old creature, with natural stores of liquids and solids and she wastes away daily becoming younger and younger, until she shrinks and disappears into thin air, leaving no refuse and producing nothing concrete or useful. It is even said that if a man is patient and persistent enough, and if he is favoured by fortune, he might one day come across a lizard as she evaporates and disperses through the air. That man acquires some notion of perfect, though useless, beauty.

Contrary to the lizard, the silkworm prospers in a damp and dark environment, under the tireless care of others, and grows like all organisms with one purpose: that is how to give the most valuable return, following a complex and particularly lucrative processing of its body.

Regardless of how successfully Zervos managed to put this method to work, he was now (on Thursday morning, a few hours before his funeral) lying still, neatly dressed in black, his face imperceptibly turning into wax. Deep inside him, secretly, beyond any means of observation, many liquids flowed out of the glands that open up only after death, liquids which in a few days would enable the rigid body to become silken and translucent. Now it has been observed that each man not only dies as he lived but is also broken down to his elements according to his occupation and his activities while alive. Hence Zervos had to undergo three changes, where one is enough for most people. Thus from the very moment of death he entered the stage of dull and inflexible soap, which was completed during the candle-lit wake in his house. When the body of the murdered man was carried and placed inside the heavily scented atmosphere of the church, everything dull and brittle began to give way and be replaced by the sheen and flexibility that only candle wax possesses.

At approximately the same hour Dikeos, who had lived his life contrary to the methods of both the lizard and the silkworm, stood up among his wild and scraggy carob trees and walked down to the town in order to conduct a sale and a purchase. Grigoris was at their vineyard, while the dead man's family were doing the final preparations before the service and the burial. It was decided that the coffin would be carried alternately by three cousins of the deceased (one of whom was the primary witness for the prosecution), two or three nephews (sons of Zervos' three sisters) and his elder son, Markos.

Zervos' only brother, five years his younger, was not present at the funeral, because he was away from the village and from Greece itself. To explain: in 1923, following the Asia Minor disaster, Zervos' brother and four other villagers emigrated to the new world, as America is called. After four years all the immigrants except Zervos returned to the village, bringing back the large sums of money they had saved from working as labourers on the railways or the roads. Andreas Zervos (that was his full name) returned in 1929 when it was said that the American currency collapsed, money lost its value and many people went bankrupt.

Georgia didn't go to the funeral either, but stayed at home because of her foot. She even took advantage of the quiet and wrote a brief letter to her uncle, describing what had happened. In two months the victim's family received a letter of condolence together with a cheque for one hundred dollars. With this money and the fifteen thousand drachmas awarded by the court Markos bought a three-acre plot of land, which started from Dikeos' big carob tree, stretched alongside the river and ended at the third waterfall. The land contained seventy five carob trees and twenty seven olive trees and was suitable for growing grain and pulses. When Zervos' brother returned to Greece and came to the village for the day, he expressed a wish to visit the murdered man's grave. Markos asked him if he wanted to see the land they had bought with his aid, but the immigrant refused to climb all the way up to the second waterfall, feigning urgent business in town, where he was staying. In the end he went back to the new world, after the economy of this far-away land had recovered.

The procession from the house to the church and then the graveyard was formed by Zervos' close and distant relatives as well as nearly all the villagers. The dead man's Liberal friends and even his political rivals (who were very few) came and paid their respects and even displayed strong emotion. It was obvious that if the dead man could have come back to life and been included on the Venizelist ballot paper, he would have gained an absolute majority, at least from their village. But nobody knows how Zervos would have reacted to this highly speculative hypothesis, which was voiced by his first cousin just before they lifted the coffin. Now as for Zervos' political influence, much was said about it in the obituary read out in church, and there is no doubt that he would have felt great satisfaction if he could have heard it. But since it is not possible to form any certain opinion as to the feelings of the dead, the only thing that could be said in this case is that, although deeply grieved, his family felt proud. They even held up the whole ceremony for half an hour to enable the private secretary of the Liberal candidate, whom Zervos represented and supported in their village, to be present at the funeral.

And so it happened: although it was the middle of the election campaign, Zervos' candidate telephoned his secretary and instructed him to go to the village and speak on his behalf at the funeral of his political ally. At half past eleven a small car arrived in the square, covered, as was common practice then, with photographs of Venizelos and of the candidate, who had served as a Liberal MP in three previous parliaments. Following the electoral victory of August 19th, Zervos' candidate (godfather to Eftychis and a doctor by profession) was appointed Deputy Minister of Health and Social Security, thus attaining one of the loftiest positions.

The secretary first conveyed the MP's sadness and deep shock at Zervos' tragic death. The MP assured them that, had the country not been in the middle of this critical election period, he himself would have come to pay tribute and brought in person the wreath he was only able to send. Also that the party had enormous confidence in the police and that he personally believed that their concerted efforts would lead to the discovery and arrest of the murderer; that a peaceful society, law and order are vital and fundamental principles of the Liberal bourgeois state; and that the government which will emerge triumphantly from the elections a fortnight on Sunday will be based on those very principles and underwritten by popular mandate.

The whole obituary could have been taken by an unbiased listener as an electioneering speech, even though the speaker, according to custom, referred many times to the personality of the deceased, as well as to his work as a good citizen and patriot during the crucial years of 1914-1916. Still, the most interesting point in the speech was the hint, heard twice by the audience, that the murder of the citizen democrat may well have been the work of a wider plot; that those who shot Zervos were aiming at undermining Greek democracy and the Liberal bourgeois establishment. It was the duty of all patriots, he said, to remain calm but also to be vigilant defenders of the constitution.

Another interesting point was that, although everyone knew that the perpetrator of the crime was Dikeos, the speaker never mentioned anyone specifically by name, either because there had been no time to brief him, or because he wanted to lend a wider dimension to the incident. However, during the first interrogation to which Grigoris was subjected as soon as he returned to the village, still hiding the empty cartridge in his waistcoat pocket, the sergeant asked him if he or his father subscribed to political views other than those held by the deceased. Although Grigoris was very worried by the fact that he had in his possession evidence of the crime, he mentioned that Zervos and Dikeos had not only both been volunteers in Venizelos' civil guard but that they had voted for the same MP since 1920, the year of the Venizelists' great defeat.

During the murder trial two months later, Zervos' first cousin, who had been impressed by the obituary, spoke of a possible political conspiracy, in reply to a leading question by the Venizelist lawyer. But neither the prosecutor nor anyone else appeared to support this view, perhaps because in the elections the liberal party had secured two hundred and twenty three seats out of two hundred and fifty in Parliament and also because the murderer's son, who was present at the trial, had voted openly for Zervos' candidate.

On the contrary, the court accepted certain mitigating circumstances in Dikeos' favour, not on the strength of his defence or the lawyer's speech but because the defendant's whole demeanour and attitude pointed them in this direction. The jury had either to accept the charge of premeditated murder, in which case the perpetrator would face the execution squad, or they had to take into account certain mitigating circumstances, such as a previous clean record, the defendant's confusion at the time of the crime, and the possibility of an accident. It even became obvious that if Dikeos had come forward willingly and immediately after the murder, and if he didn't keep explaining about the third and ninth day after death and the mourning and grief of the relatives, perhaps the fourteen years sentence would have been shorter. As for the alternative of an accident, neither Dikeos nor his lawyer claimed such a thing, even though during the reconstruction and the preliminary hearings the murderer himself had mentioned just that. But at the trial, although the presiding judge read out Dikeos' statement to him, Dikeos showed no interest in this important aspect of the case.

About Dikeos' reluctance to defend himself properly even Grigoris was mystified and he asked his father during an adjournment what the reason was for not saying that the murder had been an accident. But Dikeos, far from answering the question, began to expound upon the basic principles of a theory similar to that of the active and passive aspects of life. The accidental and the premeditated were related to the passive and active, but as there seemed to be no clear distinguishing line, Grigoris didn't understand very much. He had the same problem with Dikeos' letters from prison. Most of the time he couldn't follow his father's line of thought, although all those theories were

66

expressed very naively and usually originated from old stories which one hears often in the course of one's life. In Dikeos' case one major influence was his habit of reading certain popular magazines and his long familiarity with Kazamias' almanac. This was the conclusion reached by those who after many years came across his letters in the house of the Dikeakises.

After Grigoris was killed and when the years of Markos' exile ended with the new government of the spring of 1935 and Zervos' whole family came together again, the matter of compensation for the widow and orphans was raised once more, on the advice of the Venizelist lawyer. They filed a lawsuit and put in a claim for Dikeos' estate, which was now unprotected following the death of all the members of his immediate family. And since Dikeos' few remaining relatives showed no interest, nor were they able to become involved in litigation, especially against such powerful and experienced opponents, the disputed property was seized owing to the court's interpretation of the law.

The land containing the big carob tree and the vineyard with the little house was bought at a knock-down price by Zervos' son-in-law, Agapi's husband. The new landowner uprooted the black grape vines because large raisins weren't fetching a good price, and planted sultanas. He even persuaded the owner of the fallow field next door to sell him the land, so that in a few years' time a vineyard was created which was four or five times bigger than before. The crop increased seven-fold, due to better and more effective cultivation. But the village house and some more remote allotments of Dikeos' were bought by that same family of refugees to whom Grigoris had sold the two plots of land in the valley in 1928. These people cleaned out the old deserted house and they found, among many worthless things, a thick bundle of censored letters from prison, which contained the prisoner's most important theories.

The most interesting of Dikeos' theories was the one concerning the different ways of concealment and transformation by someone who has committed a murder and wants to avoid arrest until the nine days of mourning have elapsed, without leaving his home village. Dikeos may have learnt this method (which was discussed many times in the village cafe) when he was serving as a civil guard in mainland Greece: no other villager or any of the local policemen had ever heard of it. The effectiveness of the method was proved by the fact that, although the police and many civilians searched the carob trees and the surrounding hills more than once, Dikeos (who later confessed that he had been hiding at that very spot for nine whole days) remained completely invisible. Only when the ninth day was over did the fugitive abandon his hideout of his own accord. He sat at a prominent spot and waited for them to come and arrest him. Indeed, on the eleventh day after the murder, on Saturday 18th August, eve of the elections, the detachment finally managed to find him and arrest him without resistance as he was relieving himself under a carob tree. He asked them to let him finish and after pulling up his trousers and tightening his cummerbund, he went into the nearby hut, took the Mannlicher and the five well-polished bullets and gave himself up.

The only time Dikeos risked being caught was the morning of the second day of hiding, during Zervos' funeral. Dikeos decided to break off his concealment and come down to the main village in order to sell his ring and purchase food and tobacco for the remaining days, since the rusks he had taken from the house were by now all gone. He figured that the chances of his being recognised were very slim, even if the identity of the murderer had become known. This was because he very rarely came down to the main village, he didn't know many people or have any business there; and since all his fellow villagers should be at the victim's funeral, it was very unlikely that any of them would be in the main village that day.

So as Dikeos walked into the main village, overwhelmed by the crowds buying and selling in the market, and tried to remember the street where the pawnbroker was, another crowd had gathered in the church of his village for the funeral. Inside the open coffin Zervos had already passed from the stage of dull soap to the translucency and glow of candle-wax. The late hour, the heat of the season and the breath of so many people, the burning candles (products of the dead man's family), the effect of the August flowers (geraniums, domestic daisies and, most of all, the white lilies of the Virgin Mary) - all these things meant that the alteration of the dead body was rapid and complete. There remained the final and most important stage of turning into silk, but Zervos would go through that alone, away from the eyes of relatives and friends, inside the dark and impregnable depths of the earth.

The murderer was going through a comparable, although different alteration, as he sweated and thirsted his way round the narrow Turkish lanes of the town. But when he entered the little pawnshop he was refreshed by the coolness inside and took a deep breath of contentment. Thus he was able to explain to the dealer in precious metals (who was also repairer of watches and sewing machines, street photographer and seller of chemicals and advice for wine-making) that he was under great pressure to sell his ring. The dealer recognised the stranger's decision as a sign of extreme poverty, since a wedding ring (even a widower's) ought to stay on one's finger until death. This thought went through his head again and again as he was helping his client to take the ring off his finger. Only after a long time and with the help of a lot of soap did they manage to ease it off, leaving in its place a pinkish-white circle.

The ring was priced at a mere one hundred and ninety drachmas, which is about half a sovereign, because, as the pawnbroker explained, the metal had worn away on the man's finger in the course of all these years, and besides the purity of the gold was only moderate. With this money Dikeos bought three okas of rusks, two okas of olives, one carton of a hundred cigarettes and a good quantity of tobacco and rolling paper. For a moment he thought of buying half an oka of sugar as well, because he knew that a fugitive often craves for something sweet in the long hours of hiding and quite often this irrational craving drives him to leave his hideout and give himself up prematurely. But then he remembered that figs and grapes were now in season, in case he wanted something sweet, whereas tobacco and bread are not to be found in the fields. So he soon got back to the carob trees, although the steep road and the heat exhausted him. It was approximately the same moment as the priest was reading the last prayer over Zervos' open grave and the people were throwing handfuls of earth in it, just before they laid down the slabs and sealed the grave with clay and plaster.

In less than half an hour Zervos was left all alone and began, in the darkness and the silence, to pass from the stage of soft wax into the first phase of turning into silk. Meanwhile Dikeos, also alone, began to pick up again the rhythm of concealment and transformation which had been temporarily interrupted by the need to purchase food and tobacco. He had divided the time between August 8th (the day of the murder) and August 16th (the ninth-day memorial service) into three equal parts, corresponding to the three basic methods of concealment and transformation. Therefore, Dikeos was in a hurry to get back to his hideout as quickly as possible, so that the first and crucial part of his nine-day ordeal would not be shorter than the other two. He even thought of bringing the whole schedule forward by a day, because he had lost many hours immediately after the murder looking for a suitable place to hide, and just as many the next day by going into the main village. But in the end he decided to stick to the original plan, because he reckoned that a few hours in the space of nine days do not really count that much. And so the day of the murder (Wednesday 8th), Thursday and Friday would be spent in the way of the badger; the next three days (Saturday, Sunday and Monday, the 11th, 12th and 13th respectively) would be spent in the way of the partridge, and the last three days (Tuesday 14th, Wednesday 15th and Thursday 16th August) in the way of the stone.

It is thought by many that concealment in the way of the country badger is relatively easy and comfortable and perhaps certain hours of this period may indeed seem to be so. However, a great deal of discipline and concentration is required on the part of the fugitive, because there is always the danger that he might forget himself in the deceptive comfort of those days and betray his presence. Not only that, but because he changes suddenly from a life of freedom to the confines of a hiding place and to loneliness and hardship, it is essential that he keeps thinking about his position in space and time, never letting out of his mind either the moment of the murder or the days that follow. For the rest, the fugitive must find a cave, a hole in the earth, or a simple fissure in a rock and stay there for three days curled up on the ground. He is at liberty, however, to sleep, drink water and eat. Alternatively, if he can't find a hole to hide in, the fugitive can lie down on the bare ground, as long as he throws some earth over himself and keeps thinking of the badger. But Dikeos didn't have to resort to such a ruse, because with his knowledge of the area he found his hideout fairly easily under a big rock, beside the disputed carob trees. There he stayed for three days and nights, apart of course from the hours lost on the first and second day. He did have to go and get a drink of water each night from a spring two kilometres to the north-east, inside the boundaries of the main village. Each time, he came and went on all fours like the nocturnal badger, always taking a different path. Twice he retired behind the rock to relieve himself, at dawn on the Thursday and the Friday. Contrary to the badger's habits, Dikeos covered the faeces with earth, because otherwise there would be a risk of attracting treacherous flies and, in turn, the police detachment.

On Saturday morning 11th August, the day when Markos, the elder son of Zervos, was declaring that one day he would avenge his father's death, Dikeos brushed the soil from his clothes, walked ten paces away from his hideout in front of the big rock, stretched out on the ground and assumed the guise of a hunted partridge. Although this posture looks relaxed and simple, in reality it proves especially tiring, because the hidden man must remain for three days and nights on his back, lying on the hard earth with arms and legs in the air, thereby indicating that his body is part of the ground and his limbs are dry twigs - just as the hunted bird does. The fugitive must confine himself to taking short and furtive naps and eating as little as possible, gulping the food down quickly, thus ensuring that the sense of hunger is maintained throughout.

As for dealing with thirst, things are even more

difficult because in this position, especially in the month of August, the hunted man feels three times as thirsty as during the days of the badger. Dikeos was forced to go down to the spring every two hours, in small partridge-like steps, where he drank hurriedly, turning his head frequently, not only towards the sky but also to the left and right, making sure he was safe. In that time the detachment passed near Dikeos twice and it was fortunate they didn't have a dog with them. Otherwise the hound would have sniffed out the man easily and the camouflage provided by the bushes and the twigs would not have been able to save him.

The hardships of the partridge days were naturally a considerable strain on the murderer, but at the same time they made him fit for and worthy of the next days' ordeal. Dikeos marvelled at his own endurance, because he knew by experience that few fugitives manage to complete the ordeal successfully before giving themselves up or being caught. Most of them, disheartened and exhausted, take to the mountains where they hide with the help of friends or relatives; while others roam all over the place until they are unceremoniously arrested or get fed up in the wilderness and give themselves up. But in this case, at sunrise on 14th August, eve of the Dormition (at approximately the same time as his son Grigoris was beginning to pick the grapes and soon afterwards fall into the sleep of the oxen), Dikeos was embarking on the last and most crucial phase of his concealment, which is described as the three days of stone, dryness, and atavism. And herein lies precisely the main difference between the third period and the two previous ones. Namely, that while the murderer spends all the days entirely alone, deserted and isolated, he must, during the three final days, become one with all fugitives and wanted men of the past, and develop organically according to their example. Here, then, is how people describe what happens.

The murderer or the man hunted for some other crime he has committed, either against an individual or against the state, finds a big stone or rock on which he can lie in such a manner that every single part of his body from head to toe touches the stony surface. His body must stay firmly attached to the stone for three days, whether face up or face down makes no difference. The fugitive must have a single target and purpose all this time: to transcend, by constant and persistent stretching, the width and length of his body. Indeed, tradition relates that during the time of the struggle for independence, certain fugitive freedom-fighters, opponents of the state and men of the finest qualities and purest morals, were able to increase their body area by a quarter. Most of these men were eventually arrested, and after being paraded through the streets and tortured horribly they were finally put to death. But neither their comrades-in-arms, men of the same faith and ideology, nor the tyrannical enemy soldiers could hide their admiration at the sight of those magnificent heroes with their distended limbs and the princely translucence of their bodies. Yet the main thing for which these blessed warriors were immortalised was their enormous eyes, which covered a large part of their faces and reflected (according to all eye-witnesses) running waters. This effect is due to one of the basic requirements during the three-day adaptation on the stone, namely that the wanted man must not drink any water at all. He is, however, allowed to feel thirsty and to envisage rich and bubbling waters in his mind. That is why in the end the fugitive sees the waters inside him as perfectly real, so that they are mirrored in his eyes and remain there for a long time.

In Dikeos' case there was again no difficulty in finding a suitable stone. On Tuesday morning he abandoned the posture of the hunted partridge, shook all the soil from his clothes, face and hands, and climbed on top of the stone. As in the previous days, he had beside him the bag full of rusks, olives, tobacco and rolling paper, in sufficient quantities to last him another two days.

The first ten or eleven hours passed under a burning sun and a stillness that was unusual for that time of year. Dikeos began to sweat heavily and felt with some satisfaction the coolness of his own body. Being prostrate for so many hours, he realised at some point that he had stretched vertically and horizontally by as much as two fingers. But when at about eight in the evening the mountain dew began to descend, Dikeos felt with a good deal of disappointment that he was assuming his normal size again. What's more, during the night and especially two hours after midnight, the man grew smaller and shrank so much that he considered abandoning his attempt and giving himself up. But as the feast of the Dormition would shortly be dawning, Dikeos figured that his arrival in the village would cause great commotion, especially to Zervos' relatives who were getting ready for the ninth-day memorial service. So he decided to stay on the rock, thinking that his case was probably different or even the opposite of the independence fighters: they killed and punished foreigners and infidels, whereas he had killed a Christian and a fellow-villager, not for any national cause but for personal reasons. These are taken to be things like money lending, repayment of a loan with interest, bankruptcy and the seizure of family assets for the settlement of debts. Despite these thoughts Dikeos did obey the basic rule of the three days of the stone, that is,

the atavistic union of an individual's life with all wanted
men of the past. Due to his exhaustion, he only managed
to reach back thirteen or fourteen years into the past, to
the time when he was a civil guard and hunted down
fugitives in mainland Greece together with Zervos. It
was in those days that he first started borrowing small
amounts from his comrade and compatriot. But although
he repaid these debts (rather belatedly, as he himself
admitted), they always left behind an outstanding
balance - a product of the money-lending process. Of
course, the debt was not excessive, and the lender never
exercised particular pressure, either during the two
years of their service or after their return to the village.
On the contrary, the borrowing continued for two or
three years. By the autumn of 1920 Dikeos was reckoning
that the sale of raisins and carobs would both pay off his
debt to Zervos and leave him with something over.

If the sale of these crops had taken place before
November 1st, Dikeos' targets would have been achieved.
But he delayed picking the carobs and let the whole of
October go by in idleness. Then the disastrous elections
of November 1st intervened, Venizelos was defeated,
and in twenty days the king returned from exile. The
country's political and economic life was reversed and
the price of raisins fell noticeably. To top it all, when
father and son went to pick the carobs at the end of the
month, they found the trees had been beaten and picked.
Still, despite all this, Dikeos managed to pay three
quarters of his debt and asked Zervos to wait until
Christmas, when he would pay the rest after the sale of
the first olive oil. But the decrease in oil production, the
heavy winter of 1920 and the difficult years of 1921 and
1922 with the war, the Asia Minor disaster and the fifty
percent devaluation of the drachma, all contributed to
the borrower being unable to pay off the lender and

getting into an even worse financial situation than before. So by 1926 Dikeos' debt had trebled as a consequence of repeated adjustments to interest rates, and this forced him to sell a small plot of land opposite the Turkish cemetery at a ridiculous price. Even so he only managed to repay Zervos four fifths of the loan. Now, it is well known that only profit can bring more profit and that the increase of real property, goods and chattels obeys its own laws, the famous laws of private ownership and of gravity. According to these, assets attract one another powerfully, breed and support each other in a climate of accumulation and possessiveness. Dikeos observed, sometimes with great interest, sometimes with horror, how true this ancient tradition turned out to be. He also noticed how, even when he paid his debts to Zervos, a small amount would always remain outstanding and jump up with admirable alacrity either from the lender's head or from his papers. This meant that Zervos' powerful wealth was pulling his own feeble wealth until it was completely assimilated.

In July 1928, about a month before the murder, the debt had risen to over five sovereigns or approximately eighteen hundred drachmas. Zervos informed Dikeos that as he was marrying off his younger daughter, he had to have the money. Also that, although the coming elections were sure to be a personal triumph for Venizelos and for Zervos' candidate, he would wait to see the results and immediately afterwards celebrate the engagement. Therefore he would give his borrower until the day of the Dormition at the latest. Otherwise, he was to hand over the vineyard of sultanas and black raisins and the little house. But the murder of August 8th stopped all financial transactions between Dikeos and Zervos once and for all, because neither the victim's family nor the murderer's son knew about the dealings between the two men; and so that particular debt was never settled. Nevertheless, the fifteen thousand drachmas paid in compensation for mental distress, as well as the confiscation of Dikeos' property after his death in prison and Grigoris' stabbing, meant that Zervos' family was eventually paid in full, and more. But this was of no interest to the borrower or the lender any more. Still, it was proved yet again that a debt is paid out in the end sooner or later, one way or another, and that the accumulation of wealth which begins in someone's lifetime can actually continue even after his death. This is because the laws of private ownership and gravity are not determined by a person's transient life but by the so-called line of precious metals: gold, silver, and copper coins.

The day of the Dormition dawned and Dikeos' calculations stopped at the five sovereigns he still owed. This time he had no doubt that, even after such an effort, his body was still shrinking instead of expanding. The next ten hours passed in a torpor. The fugitive had the dream-like sensation that his body lay in water which was cascading down over a big waterfall. Then at once his body would rise to the top and fall down again with the water, keeping an even rhythm. At about six in the morning, when the priests in the surrounding villages were beginning the liturgy of the Dormition, Dikeos was floating on a piece of wood in the river near the village. The river had curiously grown bigger and the swollen waters were rushing towards the sea. Then Dikeos suddenly felt quite sure that he had grown by two or three fingers in length and as much again in width, while his face and his eyes (he could tell by touch) had grown by one sixth.

This expansion of his body continued steadily for the next thirty six hours, at the rate of about one finger

every three hours, so that by the following night, 16th
August, the fugitive had grown in width and length by
about twelve fingers, while the size of his eyes had
doubled. On Friday morning, the 17th, two days before
the elections, Dikeos got up from the rock, took the
Mannlicher, the bullets, two pieces of rusk and a handful
of olives - all that was left of his provisions - walked fifty
paces to the disputed carob trees and went into the hut.
There he rolled a last cigarette, left his belongings and
walked the two kilometres down to the spring of the
partridge to have a drink of water and a wash. After
drinking and washing first his face and then his
handkerchief, he climbed up and sat in a prominent spot
in the open and waited for the detachment. An hour later
two villagers went past, three hundred metres away,
and the murderer waved his hand as if in greeting. But
they were heading towards the mountain, not the village,
and Dikeos figured that it would take several hours
before the detachment was informed. So he stayed at the
same spot for three or four hours, during which he
largely recovered his original dimensions. When later
he went back to the spring, he realised that his eyes had
lost some of their width, although they were still quite
enlarged. He noticed a similar shrinking in his hands,
which had also lost some of their transparency. So,
whereas all that day Dikeos had been able to see the sun
very clearly through his palms, although with a slightly
reddish hue, it now appeared blurred and more intensely
scarlet. At that hour, shortly before sunset, one of the
two villagers passed again in front of the murderer, this
time heading for the village. Dikeos was now certain
that he would be arrested within two or two and a half
hours. However, by the time the news had reached the
village, the police been alerted, the detachment
assembled and various formalities which arise in such

cases dealt with, the operation had to be postponed for the following day. After waiting at his post for night to set in, the fugitive realised that there was no point hanging about in the open any longer. He went into the hut and slept until dawn of August 18th.

By then the nine days were over and people were not thinking so much of the murder and mourning. Zervos himself had already become used to the new place where, it is said, people find their final residence. But his body was still undergoing a series of changes, horrific to the human eye but not to the nature and composition of flesh itself. After all, it would be against all natural order and harmony for a body to spend so many years forming itself, collecting day by day its elements (minerals, salt, sulphur, water and humours) only to discharge them all instantaneously, without any spectacular displays, explosions, or beating of drums.

To the passers-by, of course, Zervos' grave which he himself had built six years earlier may have looked the same, even after the ninth-day rites, but inside the elements were separating as the body was being sieved within the coffin. This sifting is uniform and common to everyone without exception, to the just and the unjust alike, and it has only one purpose: the separation of the elements. Some must rise up, while others sink down, so that the bones inside the grave can turn white. This even happened with the first Irini who had died in 1908 from the haemorrhage women die of. In her case the sifting was done so well that, although the blood had soaked the body and seeped through the bones to the marrow, when they opened the grave in 1922 the skeleton was found to be as white as mastic. Then Agapi washed her mother's bones with vinegar and they put them in a wooden box, because Zervos wanted to refurbish the tomb.

Indeed Zervos took a lot of care over the appearance

of the tomb and he displayed all his skill in the construction of the cubicle for the icon of St. Eleftherios. In fact, by being opposite the rather neglected grave of the Dikeakis family, his grave made its superiority in both size and construction more pronounced. The renovated monument would have been even more beautiful if on the day when Zervos was designing the cubicle for the icon the accident with the soap and his elder daughter's foot hadn't happened. As it was, the cubicle remained unfinished until Georgia's foot had recovered and things had calmed down. When Zervos finally had the time to return to it, he discovered that the original plans had been lost. Still, the cubicle was finished and inside it went the icon of the saint who had shown his might, since his namesake Eleftherios Venizelos had returned to power after the Asia Minor disaster. And if Zervos had lived for two more weeks, he would have seen the greatest ever victory of his party.

The superiority and perfection of Zervos' grave was proved after the ninth day of his burial, the time when the body breaks away from its natural confines and like the silkworm branches out over the whole area of its own cocoon. At this stage, if the dead man is big and strong like Zervos and the grave is carelessly built and weak, the walls and slabs can crack and the body can reach the surface of the earth. But Agapi, who tended the grave daily during the first three months and weekly during the first year, didn't notice any change in the whole structure, as all these cataclysmic alterations took place deep inside the ground. The whiteness of the tomb remained immaculate, the oil lamp always lit, and the seasonal flowers on the slabs passed undisturbed through all their natural phases which begin with damp freshness and end in desiccated rigor.

During the countless visits to the cemetery and the

long hours spent tending the grave, Agapi came across Grigoris three times but their eyes never met and they never spoke. Agapi wore deep mourning for the first year, even in the house when she was feeding the silkworms, or outside working in the fields or climbing the mulberry trees. In the second year, either because the black colour of her old clothes had faded or because the material of new ones had a different shade, Agapi still wore mourning but the intensity of the black colour was clearly muted. So at Easter of 1930, when it was heard that she had become engaged to someone from the next village (where Irini the tall one had come from), Agapi put on an olive coloured dress; after two months, when she went back to feeding the silkworms, she was climbing the mulberry trees dressed in green.

Her wedding coincided with Dikeos' death in prison, but Grigoris couldn't have gone to see the bride even if his father had been alive, because of the murder. On the night of the wedding Grigoris, who had received the news of his father's death on the previous day, walked to the big carob tree, climbed up it and sat there until dawn. It was the third time that he had spent the night on the great tree since 1916, when old Grigoris had been killed and they had sold the vineyard with the wine grapes. The second time had been the night of Zervos' funeral, when there was no doubt left that Dikeos was the murderer and Grigoris could not stay in the village or in the little house in the vineyard.

It was from his grandfather that Grigoris had inherited this habit of tree climbing, and he believed that it had a therapeutic effect. That is, when men are extremely upset and their whole body is suffering from a sorrow so intense that it can lead to madness, relief is not possible unless they leave the ground and hang from or stay up in a tree or a pole or even a wooden or rope ladder. Old Grigoris often used to mention the example of men driven to maddening grief through love of God or their country, men who lived for years on a branch or on top of a pole, fasting and meditating. So, the old man used to say, although sadness is a characteristic of the wise, they too need some help, especially when they are racked by maddening grief and multiple bereavement. Because when two grievous and unbearable events hit a man at the same time, it is then that he risks going insane. If for example someone dies and his death also leaves an incurable emptiness for someone who is still alive, then this sensible living creature becomes so distressed that he is driven to madness. On the other hand if somebody dies or disappears in some other way but his loss doesn't create any particular emptiness, grief is still there but it is considered reasonable and harmless to the person who feels it. In such a case the bereaved can walk about in the world of men, full of sorrow yet in no imminent danger. But in cases of multiple mourning the only salvation lies in climbing a tree where a man can live in the world of birds and trembling foliage. And his primary purpose must be to not let his sorrow emanate from three or more causes at once, because then neither the tree nor the company of carefree birds can save him.

For these reasons Grigoris was careful on the night of Agapi's wedding not to think simultaneously that his cousin was getting married and that she was leaving for the nearby village to settle there and disappear for ever in life and in death - since women stay by their husbands even after death. Nor did he add his father's death and the vacuum it had left behind in the village house, in the hut at the vineyard and in the fields. Sitting up in the carob tree Grigoris could only think and feel sad about two things at a time: Agapi was getting married and his

83

father was dead. Or: Agapi was going far away and his father would never come back to the village, dead or alive. Sometimes he would combine the two sorrows differently, but he never thought of more than two things at once.

He had kept to the same pattern on the night of Zervos' funeral, on Thursday 9th August, while Dikeos was sleeping like a badger beside the farthest carob trees. The day of the murder and the day of the funeral had included so many events that they could easily have led Grigoris not only to demented grief but to certain ruin. The discovery of Zervos' body in the vineyard, the wake while Agapi was feeding the silkworms, Dikeos' disappearance and the recovery of the cartridge, the investigation at the scene of the crime, the first interrogation, the march and the wailing of Irini, all constituted various causes and forms of sorrow and therefore, for reasons of convenience and salvation, they had to be put into order.

The fact too that Grigoris was not able to attend Zervos' funeral, being the murderer's son, and that he had had to leave the village and stay at the vineyard all the while his father was roaming the wild mountainsides and was not there to help him with the harvest - all these and other similar things were increasing the danger to his life. This is why he was forced at four in the afternoon to walk as far as the big carob tree and climb to the top. Having secured himself on the branches, he placed the events of Wednesday and Thursday into two categories: the category of the murder, which included the funeral, the lamentations, the wake and the affliction of the oxen; and the category of banishment, which included his father's flight from justice, the police detachment, his exile from the village and the final break with Agapi's family.

In this way Grigoris spent the night in safety, hanging like a bat, while overhead passed the summer Constellations, and the Galaxy descended silently but inexorably through the pastures of the heavenly dome or the gardens of the saints, as old Grigoris called them. Dikeos' son recognised several saints from behind the leaves and branches of the carob tree: the beheaded St John the Baptist, the archangel Gabriel, St. Panteleimon of the healing waters and the Virgin Mary as she prepared to drift into the great sleep.

The second interrogation of Grigoris took place on the following day, Friday 10th. On his way back from the carob tree to their vineyard he saw the sergeant and a policeman waiting for him in front of the little house. The sergeant came straight to the point and asked him whether he had seen his father the night before, and whether he had provided him with bread and cigarettes; and he stressed four or five times that if he really loved his father he must co-operate with the police so that Dikeos could be arrested as soon as possible. Grigoris replied that he hadn't seen his father since Tuesday night and he repeated almost word for word what he had said during the interrogation at midday on Thursday, shortly before Zervos' funeral began.

But this time his position was rather more difficult and at first he couldn't explain his overnight absence from the village and the vineyard. Wandering aimlessly under the impulse of grief and spending the night up in trees seemed to Grigoris to be feeble excuses and he chose not to complicate matters. So he explained his flight as a result of fear, something which is always accepted by the authorities. In fact, since the Peloponnesian sergeant had been told of the local custom of vendetta, he was satisfied with Grigoris' explanation that he feared for his life and that was why he had spent the night in the fields.

This time the sergeant avoided asking Grigoris about his political beliefs and about his father's ideology, not only as these things were common knowledge in the village but because such a question did not assist in any concrete way in the arrest of the murderer. On the contrary, it leant to the case a dimension which was hard to pursue at the moment. Even after Dikeos' arrest, on the morning of Saturday 18th August, the eve of the elections, and although the murderer was questioned on this subject and gave a relevant reply, the sergeant judged that neither the question nor the answer was of special interest to the police, since their primary duty, that is the arrest of the wanted man, had been accomplished. But given that the pre-election climate was particularly heated that day, such a question would have been perfectly justified.

In such a political climate and amid the general feeling that the elections were going to install the strongest Venizelist government the country had seen so far, Grigoris prepared to go to the village to vote, at noon on 19th August. Before he left he had a look at the raisins strewn to dry in the sun and sprayed them with a thin solution of potassium, as it had been rather damp the previous night. The harvest had already been under way on the day after the Dormition, and during the reconstruction of the crime on Saturday 18th August Dikeos had had the opportunity, between questions and measurements by the police, to check on the work Grigoris had done and to remind him, sometimes directly and other times by implication, all about damp nights, potassium solutions and the correct drying out of the raisins.

As Grigoris approached the bench with the ballot papers he decided, for an unknown reason and contrary to what he had done during the 1926 elections, to vote openly. The polling official had got used to seeing enthusiastic supporters of Venizelos vote openly since early morning and did not order Grigoris to go behind the screen to exercise his voting right secretly as the law prescribes. He did however observe that although the lame voter carefully drew a cross beside the name of the candidate supported by Zervos and although he folded the paper rather slowly before dropping it into the box, he took away with him the ballot papers of the other parties, unlike any of the other voters. When the ballot boxes were opened in the evening some time after sunset, it was found that out of five hundred and twelve valid ballot papers from the village the Venizelists received four hundred and sixty votes of which three hundred and fourteen were for Zervos' candidate personally. The anti-Venizelist party received thirty nine votes, the Rural party ten and the Far Left three.

Those three ballot papers were deemed invalid in the second count because instead of carrying the usual cross of preference on the left of the candidate's name, they bore a mark like the letter V. It was only when the results were brought together from the whole electoral district to the provincial capital, that officials noticed that all those who had voted for the Far Left (who by the way numbered no more than a hundred and fourteen among a total of fifteen thousand valid ballot papers from the province) had marked their candidates in the same manner: a V instead of a cross.

This conspiracy, as it was called by officials of the Venizelos government, was noticed in all the electoral districts of the country. It is even said that in the following year the government of Venizelos, who had won the elections with an overwhelming majority and was seen as the peace maker and saviour of the country, instructed the legislators to draft the infamous Special Law of 1929, precisely because they had found in the whole country fourteen thousand and sixty nine ballot papers marked in a conspiratorial way and the Liberal bourgeois state had to be protected at all costs.

But as far as Grigoris was concerned, the elections and their significance ended immediately after he had voted; the only evidence that could have linked the day of Venizelos' electoral triumph with the murderer's son were the unused ballot papers which were found in his house after his death, in a bundle with the letters that his father had sent from prison.

As for Dikeos, he neither voted, of course, nor did he ask about the results of the election, having gone through a very rough time for nearly a week, in and out of prison cells and transit centres. Because of the elections, the prisoner could not be transferred to Chora and was kept in an improvised cell in the main village until Tuesday or Wednesday when he was taken to the provincial capital together with the bags of ballot papers. This rough treatment of Dikeos had already begun on the day of his arrest, when the sergeant decided that the prisoner should be taken immediately from the vineyard to the police station in the main village. He considered the safest way was the path that led from Dikeos' vineyard to the carob trees where he had been arrested, and from there to the town. In this way they would avoid going past the dead man's village during the election; but it meant that the actual distance would be increased and therefore the march would take two and a half times longer.

Having finished spreading the grapes shortly before the detachment led Dikeos to the vineyard for the reconstruction and at the end of this gloomy and pointless formality, Grigoris asked to be allowed to accompany his father to the main village. The sergeant showed remarkable understanding on this occasion too. After all, Grigoris didn't pose any risk and there was certainly no regulation forbidding the relatives of a criminal to accompany him to the place of his detention.

The march began at about noon on Saturday and lasted more than five hours, whereas it would normally have taken two to two and a half. The sergeant told Dikeos, who was not wearing handcuffs, to go through all the places he had been on the morning of the murder because, as he pointed out, he wanted to clarify some questions for himself. Dikeos seemed quite rested and refreshed after washing beside the little house in the vineyard, and he cooperated fully with the sergeant, marking with extra care and great detail all the steps he had purportedly taken ten days before.

So it became clear that the path which the prisoner and his escort were following was not in any way straight but formed either slight curves due to the contours of the ground, or perfect circles around rocks or large bushes. When the sergeant inquired why Dikeos had followed such a slow and complex route when he should have found the quickest way (as people do when they are in a hurry or being pursued), the murderer replied that by this means a man's trail is totally lost to the eyes and in the minds of his pursuers and their dogs. Grigoris was impressed by his father's reply and admitted to himself with great surprise and admiration that his father had been far more prudent than he had imagined. Although on the day of the murder and the days of Dikeos' disappearance Grigoris had walked dozens of times in his mind the distance between their vineyard and the carob trees on the mountain, he had never seen him anywhere. And when, just before the carob trees, Dikeos performed a perfect square with sides measuring thirty three paces, Grigoris finally admitted that it is impossible for a route of this kind to be detected even by someone who is walking in his mind if he advances hurriedly and in a straight line.

In parallel with all these events during the march, Grigoris had the feeling that all the time there was taking place between himself and his father a continuous and persistent dialogue which the policemen were completely unaware of. Indeed, Dikeos and his son never exchanged a word; any conversation was always between the policemen and the prisoner. But Grigoris noticed that while his father kept addressing the sergeant, giving him directions for the march, in reality he and his father were having a conversation about things that concerned only them, such as matters to do with the vineyard, their animals and the jobs that had to be done. So he too began to ask his father questions and to answer him inside his mind, with concentration but also with familiarity and devotion, as befits a son talking to his father.

This conversation lasted about four hours, which was the time it took them to get from the vineyard to the carob trees. There they halted and went inside the stone hut to have a rest and for the policemen and Dikeos to have a smoke. During this time total silence prevailed, while the subject matter of the conversation between father and son turned to the picking of carobs. Dikeos said that during all those days he had spent up there he noticed that this year their trees were full of fruit and that Grigoris must come and pick them within a month at the latest. He must not delay as they did in 1920 when they had lost the crop. And he told Grigoris to do something about the roof of the hut as it was about to collapse, being exposed to the wind and rain.

From the hut to the spring of the partridge the march

continued in the same convoluted way and Dikeos even suggested that they go back and forth to the well several times because he had himself done that, always taking a different path. But the sergeant didn't seem prepared to start toing and froing to the spring and told the prisoner to press on towards the main village. Then Dikeos asked if they could stop briefly for a drink of water and for him to soak his handkerchief.

At this point the conversation between father and son had covered everything about their property and turned to Grigoris' mother, Maria the Quiet One, who had died in 1901 at childbirth. Grigoris was asking his father persistently (while the latter was talking to the sergeant about the eupeptic qualities of the water) to tell him more about his mother; but Dikeos answered that it was getting late and Grigoris ought to be getting back to their vineyard. Having fallen fifteen paces behind the others and limping in the heat of the late afternoon, Grigoris begged his father in his mind to let him come down to the main village with him. Dikeos had no objection, but because the distance from the spring to the village had to be covered in an absolutely straight line, the policemen and their prisoner quickened their pace and left Grigoris behind. As they reached the first houses of the provincial town, the distance between them was more than two hundred metres and it was obvious that Grigoris couldn't possibly catch up with them. What's more, Dikeos had increased his speed considerably so that the policemen had to hold on to his shoulder in order not to lose him. Grigoris saw the detachment disappear down the streets, he heard his father as if for the last time shouting to him, both aloud and inside his mind, that he must go back at once.

When Grigoris reached their vineyard the sun had set and the strewn raisins had already wilted in the heat of the day. In his village the Saturday vespers had finished, the women were lighting fires for cooking, the children were being rounded up back into the courtyards and the men, all washed and shaven, sat in the coffee shops discussing the elections and the year's grape harvest. Dikeos' son opened the little house, went inside and sat on his father's bed. From the small window he could see the wild roses, the downhill slope and the road leading to the village. He passed beside the Turkish cemetery, went through the village and reached the front of the Christian cemetery. Hard by the entrance he caught sight of Agapi, dressed in black.

C

When Grigoris woke up after nineteen hours of sleep at midday on Wednesday 15th August, on the feast of the Dormition, the sun was at the highest point in the sky. For two or three hours it stood still at that point where, according to old Grigoris, the solar disc grows bigger and widens its diameter as much as four-fold. It thus manages to remain suspended in the most dangerous region of the heavenly dome and to immobilise itself like the sleeping silkworm which, while keeping its eyes closed, can see the world deeply and clearly. Then the air gets very hot and all the heat pours straight down over the earth. The result is that in different places crops and trees are burnt, water boils and the lizards stand on their tails in a shower of light, and evaporate.

Many are the explanations that people give regarding this phenomenon on the day of the Dormition. But the most important and, by Grigoris' reckoning, the most probable, went back to his great-grandfather, old Pavlos Dikeakis, and reached down to the present day's feast in the year 1928. This theory was based on the so-called analogy of the religious and cosmic systems, whereby each special day commemorates one or more of the saints and develops climatically according to that saint's properties.

Consequently, on the day of the Dormition all celestial and terrestial bodies and all creatures of the air and sea must participate in the holy sleep. The most remarkable thing is that while all these beings appear to be moving, feeding, ruminating or defecating, in reality they remain perfectly still in the great heat of the expanded sun. This theory was not meant to survive very long, since with

Grigoris' stabbing it too was lost together with all his belongings.

And so it was that, in the coolness of the month of November 1931 (after a hot summer when the production of raisins, carobs, soap and - not least - cultivated silk, had seen an increase of about seven percent against the previous year) Grigoris ended his life underneath the big carob tree and saw, with the clear vision of the dying, the loss of his own world as well as the destruction of the crop and the dissolution of the whole universe, both visible and invisible.

It is not known why Grigoris climbed to the highest waterfall, having already beaten the carob trees and gathered in the carobs forty days previously. But as Markos explained after his voluntary surrender to the police detachment in the spring of 1935, he was guided to the scene of the murder by his own voice. He also claimed in his confession before the file was finally closed, that when someone sheds human blood, he sheds his own at the same time, and that this is what happened with the Dikeakises. Of course, his own blood or his son's blood was in danger now, but because Dikeos' family was now extinct and Eftychis supported the new government and was under their MP's protection, Markos and all his kindred (Agapi, her husband and her children, Georgia and Irini the tall one) were in no danger either in the immediate or in the foreseeable future. And as has been observed countless times, what men call justice is directly dependent on an individual's possessions and relative to the laws of ownership and gravity. Consequently Zervos' family didn't experience any danger nor did it suffer any injustice.

Truly, after the death of Zervos and the destruction of the silkworms from the great downpour the day after the elections, no other loss was recorded in the family.

All that was lost was regained and even increased with the passage of time. Even Markos' words, spoken at noon on Saturday 11th August, that if he didn't kill his father's murderer he would surely kill the murderer's crippled son, were not wasted. They were heard clearly not just by all the villagers and the men who sat in the coffee-shop waiting for lunch to be prepared and by the women who were in a hurry to finish all their chores, but also by Markos himself. He heard his own voice, he said, calling him three years and three months later. In his case there occurred what has been observed in similar situations of great anger, when men become furious due to political or national or economic reasons and sometimes let out a great cry as a sign of their opposition and disaffection. Such a cry can be preserved in the air for many years, even decades, until it is harkened to by another person with similar feelings or heard again by the person who first uttered it.

On his part Grigoris heard Markos' shouts only at midday of the Dormition, shortly after he woke up and began to plan the harvest all over again. Dikeos' son didn't pay particular attention to Markos' threats, nor did he worry. On the contrary he remained unmoved and indifferent, either because of the heat or because of his long sleep. He was also idle as regards the harvest, something that he personally explained as a result of the general inertness and inactivity that prevails on the day of the Dormition.

But later it turned out that this delay cost Grigoris half of the sultana crop of that year, as the terrible and wholly unexpected August downpour on the day after Venizelos' victory washed away the strewn raisins and destroyed them. To be fair however, it should be said that this time the disaster affected not just Grigoris but most of the farmers of the region. Some of them even suffered a one hundred percent loss. So with the announcement of the final election results the Minister of Agriculture made a statement about certain measures to be taken to assist areas hit by the flood.

Several years later and after a series of economic crises during Venizelos' term of office those with a better memory and particularly people from Grigoris' province recalled the flood of August 20th, 1928. In the way people usually link such events, they pronounced that those four years of glory and power for the government had begun under a bad omen. But it is true and has been positively confirmed that the sixty percent devaluation of the drachma in December 1932 was not caused by the 1928 flood but by bad management and the speculatory tendencies which develop and flourish under this type of government. Naturally one should also take into account the international economic crisis and especially the devaluation of the British pound. From the moment England officially abandoned the gold standard and imposed the obligatory circulation of coins, one can see how an additional reason emerged for the destabilisation of the drachma and the collapse of the Venizelos government. However, in November 1931 foreign currency was still of some value and that is why the gold sovereign and the drachmas found in Grigoris' blood-soaked pocket were enough to pay for his funeral and the memorial services.

The damage done to Zervos' property was also considerable and worsened his family's position, even if only temporarily. Of course if he were alive he would easily have extracted some compensation in the form of a loan, as he had done many times in the past. But because Markos and Eftychis were not yet involved in politics and their MP was away in the capital (busying himself at the Venizelist party headquarters while he pressed his case for a position in the government) it was a long time before steps were taken to obtain a loan for the family.

For the loss of the raisins, which was no more than a quarter of the total production, Zervos' family received compensation as if they had lost half. But for the silkworms, which died from the terrible thunder during their last day of sleep, the family was compensated for only a third of their presumed value. This setback was seen by Agapi as a consequence of her father's death, because such a thing had never happened before. The silkworms had fallen asleep, well fed and tended, and had begun to find in their minds one end of their silken gut. Then the flashes of lightning and most of all the deafening thunder (which often accompany a summer storm) woke up the larvae. They were so terrified that within a short time they stopped their production, and from the glassy, useful and productive creatures they had become, they took the colour of opaque wax and they all died.

Agapi filled two whole baskets with dead larvae and threw them into the field next to the house. Then she cleared the frames of all the dry leaves and twigs, opened up the room that used to be kept closed, and whitewashed it from floor to ceiling. She did the same with the big room where Zervos had been laid out a few days before. This was something that the neighbours and probably the whole village found curious, because spring cleaning and whitewashing do not become a house which is in deep mourning. As for the production of silk, during the following years and especially the year Markos stabbed Grigoris, it increased remarkably since the climate and circumstances in general proved favourable to silkworm breeding. In addition Zervos' sons built a second breeding room next to the little one, doubling the area covered by the frames.

Thus Zervos' family prospered just like the silkworms, and did not suffer particularly from the continuous devaluation of the currency, not even when the crisis had to be officially admitted by the government at the end of 1932. On the contrary their chattels and assets kept multiplying with increasing speed, even after Markos committed the murder and Eftychis joined the police force. Because, as everybody knows, when private property and in particular capital, acquires its own power, that is, when it reaches the so-called threshold of appetite, it only needs to enter the process of increase and multiplication, and from then on it will consistently obey its own laws and methods so that its value never decreases or wears out but continually gets stronger and grows.

On the other hand, if for various reasons someone's property stays below the threshold of appetite, it needs support through constant and heavy loans, of the sort that create new debts. And when seizures or fines for lost lawsuits are imposed, this property loses its value to such an extent that the laws of ownership cannot save it nor the laws of gravity apply to it.

This was abundantly proved in Grigoris' case. When Markos stabbed him after a brief struggle, Dikeos' son ended up half in the water and half on the river bank underneath the big carob tree. So, as the stream flowed slightly swollen from the recent rains and tumbled down successive waterfalls, it carried with it a fine thread of blood. At first Grigoris tried to hold this thread with his hands but it proved impossible. So all he could do was to follow his blood closely as it leapt over each of the waterfalls, frothed up with the water and spread in circles over the depressions in the river-bed. In this way he went past all eleven cascades and after three or four hours he reached the valley and stopped.

The stabbed man tried, as many do in similar circumstances, to hold back his blood, to pull it out of the water gently bit by bit with his hands or his mind and pour it back into his veins. So with one hand he clutched the carob tree and with the other he pulled at the red thread to draw it in. But the only thing that happened was that the thread stretched to such a point that it was in danger of snapping and separating from his body completely. So he not only relaxed his hold but now, willingly, let his blood flow away from him without caring about what was vanishing forever. He curled himself up like a field hedgehog which in this position has no arms or legs showing and all its belongings are locked inside its body. Thus he easily left their big carob tree and was swept away by the river, disappearing towards the valley in a pool of blood. He left the whole field around the carob tree, and with it the field where he sowed the annual wheat and pulses. Grigoris' mind flew swiftly and circled around the valley and the surrounding hillsides and reached the lips of the cosmic funnel. First he was going to assess the value of the land that had survived all the sales and seizures; then he would move on. So he put behind him the fourteen olive trees and the distant carob trees, even if they were not theirs by deed. Next he returned to the village and stood outside their locked house.

He took the key from underneath the flower pot and went inside, into the big room with the chest, the sofa, the table, four chairs and the draped mirror. All this he abandoned easily, but he didn't dare open the chest to look at and calculate the value of the things in it. He merely recalled what they were and left them there. But he did see his mother's bed (where she had fought with the Leader of Armies), the two storage jars for the oil and the empty wine barrel. He tied all these things together with the thread of blood and they drifted away, free from the law of ownership and the great principle and power of gravity. Grigoris now met with a difficulty as he entered the kitchen, where there were objects which had once been used for cooking and eating. He stayed there for some time holding in his hands the knives and forks, the frying pans, the cooking pots, the plates and cups. He might have stayed in there covered by tea towels and table cloths and smeared with oil, cooking fat and gravy, if he didn't have more ground to cover in the cloudy November sky. So he rushed out of the kitchen window and flew high up, leaving glasses and cooking pots to crash onto the kitchen floor and break into pieces behind him .

Lying upon the ground on his back stabbed by Markos, he thought he saw himself holding the little coffee pot which, as old Grigoris had told him, came from his mother Maria's dowry. Grigoris felt happy that in his great misfortune he still had the coffee pot in his possession, although he had never used it himself. But because he was already feeling tired and pressed by those forces which, according to many, control the bodies of the dying, he dropped the utensil somewhere between his village and their vineyard; the pot became once more subject to the law of gravity and ownership and fell to the ground with a bang.

Then the stabbed man felt lighter and his blood began to flow freely. In fact he noticed, with his eyes and his mind, that this vital liquid of the human body was not running downward towards the fertile plain, but contrary to natural law it dipped upwards and, instead of forming a straight line leading nowhere, it turned first at an angle and then slowly formed an arch which led back to him. Simultaneously all other things - assets and chattels and objects of daily life - instead of piling up on the earth and lending with their size and weight the assurance of ownership and of a comfortable life, were now vanishing in an extraordinary way, as if by magic, as they all followed the non-lucrative advance of the blood flow. Within this wide compass of loss and waste came finally Dikeos' vineyard, along with all the vines, the fruit trees and everything else that the field contained.

Things looked easier at first when Grigoris reached the little house in the vineyard. Flying past high above, he surveyed the whole vineyard and the white house and he let them go out of his hands and disappear. But as he opened the door and stood on the threshold looking at his father's bed on the left and the nails in the wall with the baskets, the ropes and the bag of rusks, Grigoris felt a great pain which was unconnected with Markos' stab wound. Because when someone stabs you, it comes from outside and you can forget it in your mind and try with your own hands to close the wound, although of course this doesn't mean that you survive. But when a man enters the house that has always been his and sits on the bed where he has been sleeping for years and opens his wardrobes and his drawers, which are no longer his; when, that is, a man's house doesn't shelter him, warm him and protect him any more, it has been observed that such a man almost always feels a stabbing pain that comes not from outside but from within, from his own home. In many of these cases the law of ownership may not apply (something which, naturally, anyone is free to check, if he wishes), but the law of gravity most emphatically does.

At this critical moment, while Grigoris was suffering from internal and external pain, in his mind he begged all those powers that determine everything to do with life and death, to allow him to take the key of the house, without touching anything else, not even a nail in the wall, leaving everything where it was, secure in its proper place. But the powers who daily traverse the visible and invisible world from end to end and who (according to their own concept of justice) determine ownership, contracts and title deeds, as well as set the prices of oil, soap and silken garments, commanded Dikeos' son to leave the key on the table and draw the door shut behind him.

Grigoris didn't have the time or the strength to object so he went out at once. He did however discover that despite all this he could still hold on to all the images that he loved and that were connected with their house, with the endless days of winter and summer, with lovely mornings or difficult nights. So as Markos was entering the mountains and starting his exile, Grigoris was climbing the funnel of the world by ever-increasing circles, while far down below, the vineyard and the little white houses of the village glistened. Then the wounded man opened up his coiled body again and it stretched over the ground and rested. This happens to all who have been stabbed or shot by a Mannlicher bullet and, naturally, to those who fall off trees and spill their brains over the rocks.

But Grigoris could not have imagined losses of this kind, losses which are irrevocable, on the day of the Dormition, still half asleep on his father's bed, amid the general stillness and inertia of the universe. He still owned his property then and still strove to preserve it and increase it, something he was not able to achieve. And if eventually he let his own blood flow around the world and disperse left and right and saw all movable and immovable things lose their weight and their nominal value, this only happened a few hours before he died. Because man's nature cannot, and perhaps should not, change unless there are serious reasons for it, such as death or separation in life.

Even then nothing is absolutely certain, and the matter of ownership in particular remains imponderable and obscure. Thus we don't know whether in the case of Zervos, for example, anything changed and whether the shot man was able, during the hours he was bleeding, to observe the ascension to the sky of his own blood, or whether he was able to notice any change in the laws of ownership and gravity. What is certain however is that with the shot Zervos' cummerbund was loosened and all the money he was carrying fell to the ground. Naturally the man bent down to pick up the coins, but being fatally wounded and weighed down by the universal laws, he was not able to get up again. It is very possible that he too hovered overhead for a while, but his entire property, his money, his oil, his soap, his silk and all his earthly possessions in general remained firmly on the ground; they all carried on steadily increasing, without any of the circuitous movements or deviations that go against the law of gravity.

Anyway, regarding Zervos' hovering and the loss of his money, only the Dikeakises, father and son, could really give any specific information. The matter of the money was never discussed, even between father and son. But on Zervos' hovering Dikeos repeatedly gave information and although each time he would add some detail or keep silent on some point already known, one thing remained certain and unaltered: that the murderer not only saw his creditor clearly through the little window on the morning of Wednesday 8th August, that he not only aimed at him steadily and coolly, but that he also watched the bullet itself fly out and hit the victim in the stomach a little below his cummerbund. Furthermore, that he held the rifle at such an angle that the bullet followed not a straight course but a curve, heading towards the sky. Thus, while an ordinary bullet moves in a straight line, hits the target and disappears, the disciplined Mannlicher bullet burst out, initially also going straight, but just before it found its target it dipped upwards so that it lifted Zervos off the ground to a great height. Dikeos assured Grigoris, during their last meeting inside the cell of the police station in the main village, that Zervos followed the spiral course of the bullet and that the man did not just spin around himself once or twice but that he whirled round in the air more than twenty times. So the money-lender hovered for five or six minutes and surveyed the whole vineyard, apparently counting the vines and the grapes from above and making assessments and calculations, until finally he came back to the starting point and fell to the ground, where he was eventually found.

Grigoris' visit on Monday morning, August 20th, the day of the flood and the disaster, took place after obtaining the necessary permission from the police and lasted four hours - from seven to eleven in the morning, at the first drops of rain. Father and son had the opportunity to talk undisturbed for those four hours about all that had happened from the day of the murder, 8th August, until the time of the visit. During the meeting, the two Dikeakises not only reviewed the events of the last fortnight (by various means of compressing time and welding it together) but in their discussion they included all that had taken place between 1901 and 1928. Through constant references to the past, through triangles, squares and circles of reminiscing, they talked about events starting from Grigoris' birth and the death of Maria the Quiet One, and ending with Zervos' murder. Together with an analysis of the family history, they surveyed the political and economic life of the village and of the region and, on several occasions, of the country as a whole.

During this chronological review, Dikeos was reclining on the wooden bed of his cell, while Grigoris sat on the floor as there was no chair. All the while Dikeos would taste, one by one, the things that Grigoris had brought him and which the police had allowed in, that is, half a basketful of black grapes, a bag of rusks, olives, four hard-boiled eggs and half a bottle of wine. At first there was some problem about the wine, and the police chief (who had stayed up all night because of the elections and the vote count) seemed unsympathetic and bad tempered. But after the intervention of the sergeant, they allowed in the wine, which Grigoris had managed to find in the dark at the village house, just as the first election results were being announced, shortly after midnight on Sunday.

He had set off from the vineyard at five in the morning, having first turned over the strewn raisins, which he meant to gather up that afternoon. When at a quarter to seven he had reached the police station, the raisins were already hot under the morning sun and steaming, blond and crisp on the ground. In the four hours he was locked up with his father in the cell, the weather changed so drastically that the rain, which began at about eleven, lasted for four whole hours. The result was that it not only carried away and destroyed the drying raisins, but it also drowned many animals and awoke the silkworms in their dark room and wiped them out.

In vain did Grigoris try to explain this unexpected change in the weather, in his exhausting and weird journey back to the vineyard. In vain did he struggle to quicken his step through the rain and the wind. All he was aware of was that he kept sinking into the thick mud and that the rain was not falling in drops any more but pouring down like one of the waterfalls of the river or like watery columns, which made walking more and more difficult. He even had the feeling that he was not stepping on the earth but had found himself somewhere in the middle of the dark, indefinable sea, expecting to be drowned at any moment. So in his mind he left the muddy ground, abandoned the posture of an erect man and took the horizontal position of a swimming eel.

In this way he covered five to six hundred metres, but the vineyard with the strewn raisins was still far away and it was impossible to shorten the distance or increase his speed in the rain. Just then it seemed to Grigoris that many cries reached his ears but he couldn't tell where they were coming from or what they were saying. He had the impression, however, that these voices were urging him on and he discerned a woman's voice standing out above the rest, a voice at once familiar and unfamiliar; although it was loud, at the same time it seemed soft and quiet, like that of Maria, his mother.

So Dikeos' son stopped in the rain, perplexed, and pictured in his mind the village down below, which is said to correspond to the village up above, their own village where people lived. Now a curious thing happened, which occurs often and has to do with the communication between the two villages and their inhabitants. At that moment Maria was sitting on the threshold of their house beside old Grigoris and opposite Zervos, who had only just taken up residence. Maria stood up and started calling out to her son in the way women do. At the same time everyone down there began to urge their children, their wives and their brothers and sisters in the village above, to run and save the raisins in their vineyards, the haystacks in the fields, the drowning animals and the silkworms suffocating and dying in the midst of thunder and lightning. This happened because, as people believe, although the village below is protected from rains and heatwaves, yet those residing there are able to watch all that takes place up above, missing nothing, and they can feel every change in the weather and in time. It is also said that these people not only follow the changes in the seasons and the shifts in temperature, but they are also very concerned about the cultivation of vegetables, the sowing and the grape harvest, the gathering of carobs and olives. That was why in the hour of the great downpour those people, without getting wet (and without the least prospect of selling, buying or profiting from farming, animal husbandry or silkworm breeding), were shouting, waving their arms and rushing here and there, some urging, some begging and some, like Zervos, cursing and threatening.

Now one cannot say with certainty whether Agapi, who was inside the room of the silkworms during the storm, was able to hear her father's cries, because the noise of the rain and the continuous deafening thunder made every communication difficult, if not impossible.

As for Grigoris (something he recollected several days afterwards), he had had no doubt in the end that the cries and promptings he could hear came from Maria and old Grigoris. In fact, as he was going up the slope towards the vineyard like an eel, he could see between the greater and smaller columns of water old Grigoris' face taking shape - now shaved and rosy cheeked, though aged, now very pale, his mouth sealed with Zervos' wax and his forehead smashed and bloodstained from the fall. But although he very much wanted to, he was not able to see Maria's face among the wild tassels of rain. For it is said that a person can never see in his dream or in an apparition, even if he is in some great danger, a face he has never seen before, either alive or in a photograph.

This matter was discussed during Grigoris' visit to his father's cell, when Dikeos was asked why there wasn't a single photograph of Maria in their house, which could help the son form some picture of his mother's face. Dikeos, who had been asked the same question many times before, had at that point reached the events of the Venizelos years 1914-1916. By deftly turning the conversation, he descended to family events of the year 1901, at the beginning of November. Grigoris followed his father and went with him into the room upstairs in the big house, where Maria's bed was.

He saw the body of the woman in labour, now becoming straight and long, the slender feet reaching out of the window, now curling up like a hedgehog and sinking into the centre of the bed. But because the cotton wool and the rags were not enough to stop the woman's bleeding, the village women all around her were shouting to the men to rip the sheets into long strips and give them to the midwife. You could see the old woman struggling first of all to pull out the child (who was gradually coming down and nearly drowning in the river of blood) and at the same time hastening to stop the flow and keep it inside the room. The pot was boiling outside in the yard and hot water was being carried continuously up to Maria's room, when the midwife's voice was heard saying that the child had changed position in all the liquids and blood and Dikeos now had to choose which one he wanted, the mother or the child? Dikeos, who was feeding the fire in the yard, answered that he wanted both the mother and the child, but his words were not heard clearly amid all the shouts and the commotion. So the midwife reached deep inside the foliage and the nests of the woman and pulled out the male child, alive but damaged on one foot.

This is the moment when people say that a man is

torn in two and doesn't know which one to choose: the woman who is still only barely alive, gaping open and spilling out her last blood drop by drop, or the child who is yelling as he is being washed in the bowl? In order to avoid making a decision or even accepting what was over and final, Dikeos collected all the photographs of Maria, along with a big enlargement showing the couple together. The man was sitting on a chair cross-legged and the woman was standing beside him dressed in her best, resting one hand on her husband's shoulder. While things were taking their course in the midst of shouts and panic, Dikeos threw all the photographs into the fire, keeping the enlargement until last. He looked at the curious pose which the street photographer had given to the two living bodies so that the seated person appeared taller than the standing one. And the more he looked at the photograph the smaller Maria grew beside him and she was no longer resting on his shoulder, her face somewhere between a smile and indifference, but was already being pulled underneath the chair and sinking into the earth.

On the following day, shortly before Maria's funeral, that same street photographer was heard passing through the village advertising his technique of immortalisation through photography and declaring in a resounding voice that bodies may decay and disappear but photographs live for ever and ever. Dikeos left his wife lying all dressed up and decked with November flowers and ran quickly to bring the photographer with all his equipment into the big room where the coffin lay resting on two chairs. Then he asked the artist to use all his skill and take the most magnificent photograph he had ever taken. The photographer complained that neither the lighting in the room nor the posture of the prostrate woman were very helpful to this task. Dikeos admitted that this was so, but still he insisted on having the photograph taken, regardless of whether the result would meet with his expectations. He added that a dark photograph is better than nothing and that, irrespective of whether Maria's face was showing or not among the flowers, the photograph would preserve a body which in a short time would be gone forever.

Dikeos hid the photograph among old letters and bills for twenty eight whole years. But as Grigoris was coming out of the police station in the main village he heard his father telling him where the photograph was hidden and that he should find it and send it to him in prison. Grigoris managed to reach the vineyard after four hours and his only thought just then was how to gather his raisins out of the mud and water. For five hours he struggled to pick up one by one the soggy and half-spoilt sultanas. In the end he managed to save about half of the whole crop, and he carried them inside the house to dry out.

When Grigoris woke up next morning, the 21st, in the middle of piles of soggy raisins, a brilliant sun was emerging and it looked as if the day was going to be warm. After taking the raisins outside, spreading them out once more and spraying them all over again, he looked through a lot of old and recent envelopes and discovered the photograph of Maria, the Quiet One. But he was unable to make out clearly any feature on her face, perhaps because of the photograph's age and the bad lighting when it had been taken. What he did see was the open coffin and inside a lifeless body, decked out in the way they dress and adorn the dead. On the right, above Maria's body, Grigoris recognised his father's unshaven face, taken at an angle in order to fit it into the picture.

On the day of the trial Grigoris found a chance to ask

his father, as he was giving him a fair sum of money from the sale of the sultanas, why he had not also taken him, a day-old baby, in his arms so that all three of them could be in the photograph. Dikeos said that only if the baby could have been placed opposite his father, with the mother in the middle, only then would the photograph have any meaning and be really useful and beautiful. Because if a photograph shows a dead person on one side and two living persons on the other then it looks as if the photographer doesn't know his job, since he shows neither a sense of balance nor respect for the dead. And he asked his son to return the photograph to him at once. Grigoris, who had not been able to make out his mother's face anyway, took out of his waistcoat pocket the faded print and gave it to his father, without ever learning or wanting to know what happened to it after Dikeos' death.

Apart from the matter of the photograph which covered different periods in Dikeos' narration, what they discussed at length inside the cell was the actual murder which was committed on the morning of 8th August and changed the life of the murderer, his relatives and the victim's relatives, apart of course from causing Zervos' death. In particular Grigoris wanted to know the reasons for the crime and everything that had to do with this heinous act.

Dikeos sat up on his mattress, rubbed his right foot a little which had gone numb, and over three quarters of an hour gave his son an answer which covered the years from 1909 (the time when Prince George was appointed High Commissioner) to the few days before the elections of 1928. He scanned the period of the Union with Greece and after abandoning a straight chronological sequence entered into such local detail and geographical shifts in mainland Greece that Grigoris (who had never travelled outside the boundaries of their province) could not follow his father any more and had to stay all alone inside the cell for quite some time. But Dikeos returned to the village in the autumn of 1916, just before old Grigoris fell and died and Grigoris was able to follow him on familiar ground once again.

All the events from 1914 up to the murder (events that concerned Dikeos personally or had to do with politics, with elections, coups by generals, increases in prices of crops and national disasters) referred to and were coloured by the regulations of divine and human justice. Dikeos kept arguing that the concept of so-called divine justice operates only in conjunction with human justice, so that the former cannot exist without the latter. The conclusion from this simple reasoning is that human right is not only more important than the divine but in fact every righteous action of man is wholly divine.

Things seemed to become more complicated when Grigoris pointed out that it is not always easy to tell when a human action is just and when it isn't. His father laughed and said that it was the easiest thing in the world. When, for example, someone commits a murder and the victim does not fall crashing to the ground but instead rises high and defying the law of gravity hovers overhead for quite a long time, then the murder is absolutely just and can be called an act of divine justice. He used the example of Zervos, who rose above the vineyard and stayed in the air for ten minutes before falling and breaking the vines. But when Dikeos referred to ordinary instances of murder committed either by individuals or by the state, that is killings by the police or the army or executions of prisoners, he stressed that most of the time, if not always, these murders are unjust because the victims fall to the ground abruptly and heavily, without previously hovering overhead.

Grigoris couldn't call into question the criterion of the victim's hovering. What's more, because he fell spread-eagled himself into the river after Markos' first blow with the knife in November 1931, he had no doubt that his own death was entirely unjust. But when his blood began to hover over the valley and the mountains abolishing the law of gravity, this reasoning was overturned. But by then Grigoris no longer cared about such subtleties regarding human and divine justice.

The same reasoning had led to Dikeos' view concerning absolute right and absolute wrong and the inability of so-called divine justice to advance beyond this divide. It seems that divine justice operates only when an absolute wrong has been done, an act totally opposed to the established laws, which are no more than extensions of divine justice itself. In such cases, Zervos' murderer added, the matter is simple and no one has any doubt that the wrong-doer must be punished. But cases of absolute evil and wrong are rare, and it often happens that wrongs are committed which according to the laws are not reprehensible yet are totally opposed to the principles of what is right and moral among men. For example, a man can work from dawn to dusk with the single purpose of increasing his property and wealth; a man lends the money he makes at a high interest, buys cheap and sells dear, gets involved in party politics and attracts voters by lots of promises and bribery and so contributes to his favourite candidate always being elected and increases his own influence and the power of the so-called bourgeois establishment and the Liberal party. By appearances this man is committing no injustice or doing any absolute wrong. In a case like this neither divine justice nor the laws of the state can be applied, even if this law-abiding citizen and owner of property

113

and wealth were to come one morning to your vineyard and ask to be paid back for past loans, loans which have been repaid again and again. It is then that you have to mete out human justice personally and thus guide the hand of divine justice: keeping very calm, without any anxiety or fear, you must load the Mannlicher with your cleanest and best polished bullet and aim low in the stomach at the point where the upper body meets the lower. Then pull the trigger, and you will see the bullet with your own eyes shoot out from the rifle and direct itself towards the law-abiding and prosperous citizen. At the beginning the bullet will fly forward in a perfectly straight line, but when it touches the man it will point upwards guided by the concept of justice and lift the victim high up in the sky so that there can be no suspicion that the act of murder was unjust.

Dikeos even insisted that it is essential, and in accordance with the meting out of justice, for the murderer to walk up to his victim when the latter stops hovering and falls crashing to the ground; he must sit there for hours, if possible, and watch as the wounded man slowly but steadily loses all his possessions and power. After all, this is the only way in which the act of murder can be totally justified, otherwise it might appear pointless and even negative.

At that point, during which time Dikeos had eaten about three quarters of the food, Grigoris became worried that the discussion might take a retrogressive course again and in its progress include things like loans, interest rates, repayments, creations of new debts and mis-appropriations of property, and finally reach the murder and its consequences without coming to any conclusion. So he found an opportunity, as they were talking about the vineyard and the damage that Zervos had done when he fell, to mention in great detail how he

114

had managed to pick the sultanas on the day after the Dormition, how many basketfuls he had spread in the sun and how many okas of raisins they could expect to make. At the same time he gave a full report to his father of all the days during which Dikeos had been on the run. He filled up, day by day and hour by hour, the time between Wednesday morning 8th August and the present hour when they sat talking inside the cell, Monday 20th, without however referring at all to the sleep of the oxen or the inactivity of the day of Dormition.

Nor did he refer to Markos' shouts which were heard in the great silence of that day, although Zervos' son had actually called out four whole days earlier, on Saturday 11th. Grigoris didn't know this last detail, but it was a fact that he was woken up by Markos' threats and curses and this proved very useful to the sleeping Grigoris because it was the only thing that brought him back to the world of humans, of animals, of cultivated and fallow fields and of all things in general, animate and inanimate.

He got up from his father's bed and went out of the open door into the still and transfixed sunlight. Everything around him was motionless: trees, plants, house animals and field animals, butterflies and insects, even the restless and cunning lizards. He himself had the impression that although he was walking, he stayed on the same spot. But at the same time something inexplicable was happening: he was actually moving away from the vineyard and he found himself sitting on the black rock that killed his grandfather. He thought of the rock like this because the old man may have fallen on it, but for him it was the rock which killed him and smashed his brains out. He felt annoyed that it was still standing there, an unpunished and indestructible murderer.

For his part, Markos assured everyone in his accounts

and statements before the file of the murder was closed, that when he saw Grigoris sitting on the black rock three years and three months later, he heard the son of his father's murderer calling out to him from underneath the carob tree in a provocative manner, taunting him. Thus his crime appeared to have been wholly unpremeditated and the impression was formed that he had been abused and provoked and that he did what he did in a fit of anger. But the causes of the murder were not important any more, since the pardon had been given and the whole affair had long been forgotten.

Nevertheless on the day of the stabbing and for several days later there was some turmoil in the village, although less than in the case of Zervos. Neither Eftychis nor any other friend or relative of Markos' was accused of complicity or responsibility for the murder. But it is certain that quite a few close relatives of the murderer were kept under surveillance for a short time. Grigoris was carried to the village, tied cross-wise on the back of a donkey, by that same cousin of Zervos who had been the main prosecution witness at Dikeos' trial.

Around Christmas of the same year the affair had almost been forgotten and the only thing that reminded people of it was Markos' disappearance. Two days before the end of 1931 Eftychis received a message from his brother telling him to come to the chapel of St Marina, which was situated a little higher up the mountain than Dikeos' carob tree. The meeting took place on New Year's eve, at a time when most people are gathered inside their homes due to the tradition of spending the turn of the year together and also because of the extreme cold that usually prevails during those days.

The two brothers exchanged information which they considered useful, concerning the household and its upkeep, as well as Markos' future. Eftychis handed

Markos a bundle of clothes and two bags of food and sweetmeats. His brother gave in exchange two sheepskins, thus underlining his new occupation up in the high mountains. But the main purpose of the meeting was to try and find a way of securing an amnesty for Markos through the intervention of their politician who was still supporting the Venizelos government. But because the whole political and economic situation had deteriorated during the autumn of 1931 and the country faced the danger of bankruptcy, due mainly to foreign borrowing, most of the ministers including the Deputy Minister of Health were concerned primarily about their own and the government's future. Indeed, when in September and October 1931 Venizelos was going round the capitals of countries which had advanced loans, begging for further credit, several local party activists and officials in Zervos' district expressed their anxiety and their complaints to the Minister. These people were probably not very articulate during their meeting with the government official, but they did manage to say (using phrases at times elaborate and at others crude and colloquial) that there were rumours that their MP and Deputy Minister was flirting with powerful financiers of the conservative party.

In May 1932, immediately after the resignation of Venizelos' government, Zervos' MP, after fifteen years of faithful service to the ideals of the Liberal party, deserted to the opposition's camp. In the next elections, in September of the same year, he was elected as a representative of the Populist party, gaining the support of a large part of the old Liberal vote. The voters' change of allegiance became more widespread the more Venizelos' power diminished, as the two unsuccessful coups of 1933 and 1935 showed.

As has often been observed in such cases, the voters

who switched to the other side showed excessive zeal in their new persuasion, so much so that the disagreements with their former comrades took on the dimensions of real hostilities. It was just such an incident which gave Eftychis the opportunity to actively prove his devotion to the new order of things, when he took part in the vicious beating up of a Venizelist party official.

Three months after the incident, in November 1934, Eftychis was recruited into the police force. Meanwhile Venizelos and his friends were threatening the Populist government and conjuring up the vision of an avenger sent by destiny to reinstate the Liberal party to power and save the endangered democracy. In May 1935 Markos took advantage of a sort of amnesty issued by the government after its victory over Venizelos and surrendered to his brother. When the democratic constitution was finally overthrown and the monarchy restored, Markos hung an enormous photograph of the king on the very nail where Venizelos' photograph used to hang, in the big room where his dead father, the old Liberal party activist, had been laid out. The king, unlike his picture on the gold sovereigns and the various other denominations, was facing straight ahead and gazing a little higher than normal.

Still, regardless of the political changes that took place during the time that Markos was a fugitive, he was in frequent and regular contact with his brother and with other members of the immediate family. The police never bothered any of them. The communication between the two brothers was only interrupted while Eftychis was assembling his credentials to apply to the police force, one year before Markos surrendered, when he had to show that the man who shortly would be a guardian of the law could also respect it. But after the happy conclusion of the whole matter, with the rehabilitation

118

of the murderer into society and his arrival at Zervos' house with his wife and his son Manolis, relations between the Zervos brothers became closer and the help each gave to the other more fruitful. From the time Agapi and her husband left the village of Irene the tall one and came to live in Zervos' village the two brothers and their brother-in-law acquired more and more power due to their healthy finances as well as to their ties and connections with the authorities.

Neither Dikeos nor his son Grigoris ever managed to create such a strong family. On the contrary one can easily see an accelerating decline in Dikeos' family fortunes within three decades, from 1901 to 1931. This painful truth did not appear to have a negative effect on Grigoris, who, after his father's death in prison, slept and woke up, ate and drank all alone. While his father was still alive, Grigoris apparently nurtured some hopes, albeit improbable and irrational ones, that one day the prisoner would come home and sit at the table with his son; so he refused to cook and eat properly. Instead he broke further and further away from the habit of a properly laid table with a hot meal.

When news came of Dikeos' horrible death from copper disease and all hope was lost, Grigoris at first refused to eat or drink anything for two or three days but then killed the largest rooster among the fowl that fed in and around their vineyard. He made a big fire and cooked the bird in oil with lots of spices. He laid the table, sat and ate the two wings, the neck and the head of the rooster, and buried the rest of the meat in a corner of their vineyard. But soon Grigoris recovered his old rhythm and was not interested in food, whether roasted, stewed or boiled, nor in gravy or cooking smells. Not only did he not long for a laid table, for plates and cutlery, but he created his own diet, which one could place somewhere between the food of a lizard and that of a field hedgehog: that is, the ability to get nourishment solely and exclusively from the air and the earth.

This attitude of Grigoris towards cooking and eating at a properly laid table continued until his death in November 1931. By this time the economic depression had reached such a point and the state machine seemed so incapable of reacting to it, that the signs of imminent collapse were already visible. As figures show, from 1932 until March 1933, when Venizelos' first coup took place, unemployment had reached the amazing level of three hundred and fifty percent higher than it was in 1928, while exports of raisin had decreased by fifty percent and of oil by twenty two percent.

Grigoris didn't live to see either the first or the second coup, or the subsequent bankruptcy of the democratic system and the imposition of a dictatorship. But it is not likely that these changes would have affected his diet or general way of life or even his political convictions, although such changes are natural for people who see their personal and social life take a turn for the worse. This is what happened with Dikeos, for example, who suffered a lot during his term in prison and saw many changes in his diet, in his body and in his political views. Concerning the latter, Grigoris received substantial information from his father's fellow-prisoner who visited him often after his release, each time on a different pretext and with a different excuse, but always in his capacity as a pedlar.

This strange yet extremely able tradesman, a victim of the 1929 Special Law passed by the Venizelos government, had had no education to speak of, as he admitted each time. But he gave several lessons, first to Dikeos and then to Grigoris, on the economic and social system he believed in. However the only thing that

Grigoris managed to learn in the end was the significance of certain strange symbols or cryptic signs which Dikeos used to put in his letters, and particularly what that 'V' meant with which the prisoner ended all his letters. Until the day of the pedlar's visit Grigoris had never known anyone who had gone to prison for reasons other than theft, rustling, murder or other violence - the political differences between the supporters of Venizelos and the conservative party had sent many before the courts but no one to prison. Although the political prisoner gave Grigoris some information of a general nature, he was in the end unable to describe the atmosphere inside the prison and his special relationship with Dikeos. And since the ex-convict's analyses included events and places very far away from Grigoris' village and province, his mind could not travel to those distant lands of men speaking in foreign tongues in a cold climate, and the strange food eaten by the revolutionaries of Mother Russia (a favourite expression of the pedlar's).

The last meeting between Grigoris and the itinerant tradesman had been planned for October 1931 and concerned the sale of the carobs and the whole year's crop of pulses. Grigoris had decided to purchase a rifle, something which may have been a result of the pedlar's endless stories about revolutions, armed conflicts and bloody disturbances. As initial capital he would use the sovereign and the nine drachmas he still had from Zervos' money. But for unknown reasons the otherwise punctual pedlar didn't come to the vineyard and the sale of the farm produce did not take place. Furthermore Grigoris' death four weeks later put a final stop to any plans and destroyed any hope which the Dikeakis family may have had either to see their rifle return home of its own accord or to buy a new one.

Yet even if Grigoris' dream could have been fulfilled,

it is wholly uncertain whether the rifle could ever have been used to any purpose. Because it is well known that only those people who sleep on their rifle and touch it and caress it morning, noon and night are, in the end, capable of using it. Also, the owner of the rifle must recall and recite day, noon and night all the wrongs, persecutions and economic disasters he has suffered. He must avoid uttering empty curses or wishes and must not grieve or sigh so as to cloud his mind. Most of all, he must think only of himself and, plan and act as if he embodied everyone else. But he must not use others as an excuse, nor must he invoke the common interest for actions which concern only himself. Because a misfortune should not be measured by the suffering or the grievances it causes but by the specific concrete reactions of the sufferer.

These may have been the last words that Grigoris heard from his father, as he was hurriedly leaving the cell in the main village, just as the rain began to fall. His father very probably continued talking all the while Grigoris was struggling, now as an eel now as a human being, to pass through the successive walls of rain and be back in time to find their raisins intact. And because he had no other thought but how to save the crop and not see his pains wasted (as, after all, every man in that farming district did), he was not concerned any more about his father's instructions, in the midst of thunder and lightning. Moreover the cries of the people in the underworld were sounding in the rain and the wind and confusing his hearing, and this meant that the very loud orders and howls from Dikeos elicited no response from Grigoris.

Those who did hear Dikeos were six policemen, the sergeant and the officer in charge of the police station who was asleep. When the guardians of law and order recovered from their first shock, the officer was furious at being woken up so rudely. So they all rushed inside the cell to make the murderer shut up. One was ready to gag his mouth, another to beat him up (as is common practice in such cases), and all of them to threaten and curse. But just then the eight men of the force came face to face with a strange and totally inexplicable phenomenon which, as people related later, petrified them all.

To explain: they were quite certain that they could hear Dikeos expounding in a very loud voice, which reached the pitch of a scream, how one should take aim at one's victim, how to direct the bullet at the correct angle and how to make the stricken body hover and circle above a vineyard or field. But as they came into the basement cell they discovered, in terror and amazement, that the prisoner was reclining on the bed, asleep, while his screams were making the walls vibrate. As they came and stood above his head, Dikeos was explaining, in the loudest voice a man can produce, the best way to look after a rifle so that it is always ready to fulfil the purpose for which it was made; how one must rub and polish the bullets, especially those of the military Mannlicher, so that it kills instantly and at the same time upholds its reputation for humaneness.

This strange and tiresome occurrence lasted for about an hour, while the prisoner, fast asleep, continued to scream and the policemen, driven to distraction and scared to death, stood paralysed and had no idea what to do: should they wake Dikeos, or let him sleep undisturbed, his head resting on his folded arm, meek and peaceful in all other respects? One thought followed another and nobody could make any decision or explain the situation. Meanwhile the rain outside continued to pour down, in unison with the sleeping prisoner's cries, his swearing, his scathing curses upon the state and his violent and terrible threats against its representatives.

Beyond the annoying situation which the policemen were witnessing and their obvious impotence to resolve it, there was the danger of Dikeos' cries being heard in the nearby houses and creating even more problems. Fortunately the downpour and the fairly long distance between the police station and the houses meant that the prisoner was not heard. Besides, Dikeos woke up an hour later of his own accord, and the terrible cries miraculously stopped at once. In his turn, the prisoner was alarmed to see all eight men inside his cell. But the chief of police reassured him and, after withdrawing with his subordinates, gave strict orders that none of them should disclose what had happened or make any reference to it. The incident would indeed have remained completely unknown, had one of the policemen (who was discharged after Venizelos' coup in 1933) not confided it to his family, who in turn spread the story all over the place.

But by then both Dikeos and his only son Grigoris were dead and most probably sitting amongst the rest of their family in the village below, indifferent to this kind of thing. On the day of the incident, however, even if Grigoris had been made aware of the goings-on, he could not have appreciated them fully in his panic and haste to pick up the muddy raisins and save what he could of their property. Besides, there was the precedent of his own sleep on the eve of the Dormition, when he was able to hear clearly all the voices and sounds produced by every animal or plant as it feeds, defecates or moves. He even had the impression that all the time he slept, from the afternoon of the eve of the Dormition until midday of the feast, he was far away from their vineyard, perhaps behind the mountains of his village, at the ridge of the cosmic funnel or in the regions of the constellations, accompanied by old Grigoris who was explaining yet again things well-known and often-repeated.

So while everything in his sleep seemed tranquil and bright, while the heat of the day could not burn him and everyday problems could not bother him, deep inside he felt he must hurry because time was running short and their vines were still unpicked. Outside, the basket stood abandoned with its grapes wilting in the sun, now spoilt and useless. For this reason, as soon as he woke up just before midday of the Dormition, the only thing he wanted was to come out into the light and carry on with his work. And so it was: he picked up the basket from the ground together with his bill-hook and made two or three attempts at picking the grapes, in the stillness of the day. But it seems that the only thing he managed to do was walk further and further away. Although he had the impression that he was moving around the vineyard picking grapes, in reality he was climbing high up as far as the big carob tree, holding the basket in his hands.

There he sat on the black rock until the sun went down and the stillness of nature came to an end. On the day after the Dormition, at about four in the morning, he washed in the river, left the carob tree and walked quickly down to the vineyard. He took out of the house the big bucket for diluting the potassium and filled it with water. Then he found the bag of potassium and dissolved just enough to dry out their raisins properly. After that he took the basket and began to pick the vines carefully one by one, collecting all the grapes that had fallen on the ground so that there was no waste. At that very moment Agapi was throwing fresh mulberry leaves to the hungry silkworms, and the larvae were greedily and noisily consuming large quantities of green leaves, one day before their final sleep.

June 1980 - March 1982 Athens - Melos - Athens

CHRONOLOGICAL TABLE
of main events in modern Greek history

1453 Fall of Constantinople to the Ottoman Turks, followed by mainland Greece and most of the islands.

1669 Crete falls to the Turks.

1821 Revolution leads to independence of parts of Greece and the imposition by the Great Powers (Britain, Russia and France) of a monarchy under the Bavarian Prince Otto.

1862 Otto is forced into exile and in 1864 the crown is handed to the Danish Prince George (I).

1895 Cretan revolution is crushed and in 1897 Greece is defeated in war with Turkey. Crete becomes autonomous under Ottoman suzerainty and Prince George of Greece is appointed High Commissioner.

1910 The Cretan Eleftherios Venizelos becomes Prime Minister of Greece and begins programme of Liberal policies on land reform, education, local government, trade unions etc.

1912-13 Balkan Wars: Greece regains territories in Macedonia, Epirus, Thessaly.

1913 Union of Crete with Greece.

1915 Beginning of the "National Schism" : Venizelos (i.e. the Liberals representing reform and support of the Entente in the First World War) against King Constantine (i.e. the conservative Populists/Royalists identified with neutrality or open support for the Central Powers (Germany and Austria)).

1916 Venizelos sets up a provisional government and army in Thessaloniki. The king goes into exile, succeeded by his son Alexander.

1917 Venizelos Prime Minister of a re-united Greece. Entry into the war on the side of the Entente. Progressive reforms continue.

1920 Treaty of Sevres gives Greece the administration of large areas of Asia Minor, and sovereignty over Thrace and the Aegean islands. King Alexander dies, Venizelos loses the elections and goes into exile. King Constantine returns.

1922 Asia Minor Disaster: Greek army defeated, burning and plunder of Smyrna, huge influx of refugees into the mainland after exchange of Greek (Orthodox) / Turkish (Moslem) populations. Execution of 'the Six' found responsible for the disaster. King Constantine abdicates in favour of his son George (II).

1924 Monarchy abolished by plebiscite.

1925-26 Military dictatorship.

1928 Venizelos again elected Prime Minister.

1929 'Idionym' law passed, making any attempt to undermine the existing social order illegal.

1933 Venizelos defeated, failure of military coup by Venizelist officers. Venizelos wounded in assassination attempt.

1935 Failed Venizelist putsch, Venizelos exiled to France.

1936 King George returns, Venizelos dies in exile. Dictatorship of General Metaxas until German occupation in 1940.